THE BO(
BOOK

By

Jamie
Brindle

Jamie Brindle

The Bound Book

The Bound Book

ISBN 978-1-4477-6576-9

CONTENTS

Jamie Brindle

For Mum, Dad, Dan, and Nan.

Introduction

Thank you for buying this copy of The Bound Book.

Perhaps the name needs some explaining, depending on how you got to know about it. This is the companion volume – the larger, more complete volume – of The Free Book, a book which had a hundred copies printed up, and which was given out to friends and left on buses and trains and so on, with the idea that it belonged to no-one, and could be passed from hand to hand, the movements of the copies being recorded on a website, http://thefreebook.moonfruit.com/

This one's called The Bound Book because, unlike The Free Book, this one is now bound to you.

This book contains two of the three stories found in The Free Book (the third story in The Free Book, The Fall of the Angel Nathalie, will, I hope, shortly be available in its complete form as a separate publication); this book also contains eight other stories, and a poem for free.

The Big Deal is included, and you can find Quince here in his two sequels, too.

The remaining stories are a mixture of horror, fantasy, slightly scientific fiction, and one rather straight piece that I felt I wanted to include for variation.

I hope you enjoy them.

JB, Warwick, June 2011

The Big Deal

He started by telling them how they would die. Sometimes, he thought that selling deaths was all his job really was.

It was always good to start with the death. That's what the customer was invariably looking for. That's what really *sold* them.

Having described how his client would die, Quince would then go on in a rather matter-of-fact way to explain other notable features of the life he was hawking: childhood joys and traumas (as well as any exceptional neurosis that would result from them), love affairs, major accidents, famous things they would achieve, and so on. He would then finish off by displaying a rather nice rendering depicting a trans-temporal image of the body to be inhabited, tilting in holographic increments through infancy, childhood, adolescence, and so on until after ninety degrees to old age and death.

He would then look at them levelly and ask them: *so?*

Quince had never lost a client yet.

He had never lost a client. They always said yes. Not a single time in the whole of his existence – although he existed in a place where there was, technically, no time – not one single time had he even had to offer up a second life for perusal. The Poor Souls always snapped up what he had to give them.

Quince used to wonder if these Poor Souls were the only type. Certainly they were the only ones he ever came across. They were so empty and pitiful, these Poor Souls, these clients of his, so light. Of course, there was no sight here, just like there was no smell, taste, sound, warmth, cold, or anything else at all, not even any time. And yet, were he asked to describe the Poor Souls, Quince would not have been at a loss for so much as a moment. They were symmetrical without having a shape. They were luminescent without having form or light. They were humble without having a self to humble. But, above all, they floated. Above all, they were light.

It came to him one day, as a revelation, that they were Poor Souls not because they were to be pitied, but rather because they were not rich. The Rich Souls – if they actually existed - never came to him. His job was to provide the Poor Souls with a means of gaining weight – he assigned them a life in which they might be forged into something with shape and purpose. Existence here was not a life-affirming experience. Only *life* was one of those.

This was a typical example of Quince's work:

"Hello," he would say, his awareness lightly skimming the life he was about to offer to his newest client.

"Hello," would come the reply, a faint tepid breath.

"Well, how can I help you today?"

"Existence, please,"

"Oh, existence is it? Jolly good, jolly good! Well, we have this rather splendid life just in, let me see, I put it down here a moment ago...Ah yes! Now, what have we here..."

He would then go through the motions, acting as if he were perusing the life for the first time.

"Yes, this one's a real winner," he might exclaim, "Real first class death. That's what you should look for in a life, you know, a real top-of-the-range death."

"Really?" The Poor Soul would whisper.

"Oh, absolutely, no question!" Quince would reply with feeling, "Very character forming event in your average life, death. Very important."

Here he would lean forward – even though there was no space here, he would lean forward – and try and intimate himself with the (usually slightly bewildered) Poor Soul.

"You know, between you and me," he would say conspiratorially, "Between you and me, there are some Souls that choose quite ridiculously mundane lives, purely on account of the fantastical deaths which they know wait for them at the end."

"How fascinating," the Poor Soul would reply, obviously impressed.

"Oh yes! Take this life, for instance. Well, it ends when, in the midst of bitter recriminations, your divorced partner decides they can control their grief no longer and plunges you both into the blades of an automated farming contraption! Just imagine that, will you?"

"I can't" The Poor Soul would sadly reply.

"Well, of course you can't!" Quince would be enjoying himself by now, "Not now you can't – but if you take this life, then you'll be able to..."

The Poor Soul would be all too eager to jump for the life at this point, but Quince liked to play things out a bit.

"And if that isn't enough, then how about this?" he would leaf quickly through the life and find something that seemed half-interesting, "You don't loose your virginity until you're forty – forty! – but when you do...well, look at this!"

He would lean closer and show the life to his client.

"What is this?" the curious Soul would ask, perhaps slightly alarmed.

"They are quite common in the time when you will live, I am given to understand."

"And this?"

"Horns, I believe."

"And also this?"

"It appears to be a very small species of fish. Although quite what it's doing *there* is anybody's guess."

"Ah."

"Although, of course, *you* don't have to guess. *You* could *find out!*"

The Poor Soul would be nuzzling towards him eagerly by now. A no-sale would be out of the question.

"And then there's the way you find out about your *real* parents, I mean *wow...*"

And on Quince would go, until he grew tired of his sport, and allowed his client to pass through the life he held out, unto what lay beyond.

Quince liked his job, and was never lonely, despite the complete absence of any real company. In fact, this was one of the reasons he enjoyed it so much. Here he was the exception. Next to the Poor Souls he was a real standout, something special, something different. Here he was a Big Deal.

Occasionally he would wonder if it might not be nice to have a change; sometimes he even found himself pondering a life with an almost personal interest, wondering what it would be like to experience first-hand some of the things that seemed to go on in them. He had always held the opinion that life was almost certainly overrated, and probably something of a fad. But as non-time wore on, he began to wonder more and more whether he could perhaps be wrong. After all, he had never had any complaints...

One day – or night, or at any rate, instant – a most curious thing happened. Quince was perusing a life he had picked at random from the apparently infinite mass of them which jostled forever just below him. He had observed the death first, as usual, and had been mildly amused to see it involved a religious element of frightfully complex, vaguely hopeful, and magnificently erroneous conceit. After this he had leafed through the layers, seeing nothing more of particular note, until he was stopped short by a component that inspired in him a most unusual feeling.

The component was nothing special in itself – a simple pair of shoes carrying a battered look and bearing a distinctive gold stripe down one side.

The feeling it brought about was the worrying thing.

It was a profoundly strong and inescapable feeling. A feeling of utmost weight and undeniable truth.

It was a feeling of simple, absolute recognition.

Quince was shaken to his core. This had never, ever happened before. Although, when viewing a life so that he could describe it to his client, he was somehow instinctively aware of all that went on in them, nothing had ever before seemed to him to contain any personal relevance. Usually, it was as if he had a vast and automatic encyclopaedia splayed open in the centre of his being, something that transmitted to him every nuance of meaning in the lives he held. This was different. This was an item he recognised without its essence having to be translated for him.

"Those are shoes," he thought, "You wear them when you go outside. They feel good at the front where the tips have been broken in, and sometimes the back scuffs your ankle and the skin chafes away and you bleed. You buy them at a discount price from a market because you think your friend would like the gold striped design, but then keep them for yourself because you find you like them, too."

It was an unsettling feeling, for the most part.

For the most part, but not entirely.

He put the life to one side, and often retrieved it when the desire struck him. He leafed through it with a strange, almost guilty pleasure that had barbs and hurt him almost as much as it pleased him. He lingered over it, searching in vain (and also with trepidation) for something else he might find similarly familiar. But he found nothing. Or rather, the only other odd thing he found about the life was a strange *lack* of something. There were things in it that he could not understand, and this was most unusual and worrying. It was as if the internal encyclopaedia he kept was failing when it came to this life. Worse, it seemed that this fallacy was growing – for he would swear that, when he had first looked at the life, he had understood the death with which it would end. He remembered thinking it absurd and pointless, but also understanding something of why it was done.

Now he could not fathom it.

He pondered the death most of all.

A Poor Soul came to him, as they always did.

Quince had been studying the life again, the troubling life with the familiar shoes, and had not been aware of the Poor Soul's approach.

14

He started, and then hurriedly pushed the life he had been perusing away into the distance.

"Hello, yes?" he asked, rather irked at having been disturbed.

"Hello," said the Poor Soul.

"Well, what can I do for you?"

"I'd like a life, please."

"Ah, very well," Quince reached out and grabbed a life at random. He held it out for the Poor Soul.

The Poor Soul looked a little uncertain.

"Um," it said.

"Yes?" asked Quince, acidly.

"Um, is it a good one?" the Poor Soul enquired meekly.

Quince was dumbstruck for a moment. This was not something that he was used to, a Poor Soul questioning the life that he offered it. But then, he thought, maybe he had neglected to give the life the spin he usually enjoyed presenting so much. Quickly, he glanced into the life, meaning to find a few succulent morsels there with which to tempt his client. But to his surprise, he found that much of the life had become quite opaque to him. He could see what happened in it, but he could understand very little.

"Oh, yes," said Quince, stalling, "Yes, quite a remarkable life, this one..."

"Well, what happens in it?" asked the Poor Soul, politely, but with what Quince considered something of an inappropriate firmness.

"Oh you know..." said Quince vaguely.

"I'm afraid I don't," replied the Poor Soul

"Well, you...die on a ship," said Quince at random.

"On a ship?" said the Soul.

"Yes, a ship. At sea. In a storm."

"Oh." The Soul seemed thoughtful for a moment, "Is that much fun?"

"What? Oh yes, tonnes of fun!" said Quince, somewhat annoyed by the Soul's cheek. He offered the life up to the Soul with what he hoped was an obvious finality.

But the soul did not take it.

After a moment, Quince shifted.

"Does there seem to be some kind of problem?" he asked coldly.

"Well the thing is..." said the Soul nervously.

"Yes?" prompted Quince.

"The thing is, I...don't think I'd like it."

"What!" exclaimed Quince, positively flabbergasted by now, "Well, I mean, what's not to like? I mean, it's the Sea! It's got it all! Power! Romance! The raw savagery of nature!"

"It doesn't really do it for me."

"Doesn't really do it for you?"

"What about that one, there?" said the Soul suddenly, indicating the life Quince had been looking at earlier when the Soul had arrived.

"What, this one?" asked Quince, guiltily.

"No, not that one. The other one. No, not that one either. The one you keep sort of pushing away."

"Ah, you mean this one," said Quince, reluctantly bringing out the life that contained the familiar shoes.

"Yes, that's the ticker. What happens in that one?"

"Oh, very boring life, this one," said Quince, a little too quickly, "Not much happens in this one at all. Bit of a *wasted* life, one might say. Bit of a non-event. No, you're much better going for one of these nice lives, over here."

"Hmm…" The soul sounded worryingly unconvinced.

"Well hurry up, hurry up, I haven't got all of eternity, you know!" said Quince, quite untruthfully.

"Actually, if it's all the same to you, I think I *will* go for that life."

"Well, as it turns out that life is…" Quince thought desperately, "That life is, uh, reserved."

"Reserved?"

"Yes, reserved. Here, take this one."

And he moved smartly forward and thrust a different life at random into the soul. Both Soul and life promptly vanished in a puff of nothingness.

The really strange thing was, Quince could not say for the life of him why he had done it.

After that, Quince was much more careful in the way in which he dealt with the Poor Souls. He made sure the familiar life he had found was always well hidden when his clients came to him. And he redoubled his salesmanship. The only problem was, he found he could hardly make any sense of the lives at all any more. They were growing ever more clouded to him, and he was reduced to spectacular bouts of lying when questioned on any aspect of them. Then again, he got rather good at this, and soon began to find it easier, he thought, to invent something from scratch than it was to undergo the restrictions placed on him by mere embellishment.

He pondered the irritating Poor Soul which had had the rare nerve to test his patience; but no more like it appeared, and gradually he began to forget about this strange occurrence.

Also, he was increasingly obsessed with the familiar life. He found that he could not go long without the desire to look at it growing quite sharp. But now when he looked into this life, there was virtually nothing in it at all that he could understand, although he became more and more convinced that he was recognising elements contained within. Almost everything in the life now seemed at once achingly familiar and nauseatingly arcane.

This life became both his torture and his salve; and his existence, which was technically infinite, collapsed inwards and wrapped itself in knots around the two of them, this familiar life and him.

And it was while he was in this strange state of mind that a most singular thing happened.

One of his clients came back.

It was unsatisfied.

He had been aware of the Poor Soul approaching, and had, as was his wont, hidden the familiar life carefully before it arrived.

"Hello, there," he began, as usual.

"Hello again," said the Poor Soul, with a strange infliction which Quince finally recognised as something between fear and determination.

"Er, have we met before?" he stammered, unnerved at the thought of a Poor Soul that was rich enough to carry emotion.

"Yes," replied the Soul, "I was here a while back. You gave me a life, I don't know if you remember?"

"Um, well, I give out rather a lot of those, you see," explained Quince apologetically, although, of course, he thought he knew exactly which life the Soul was talking about. Quince had never come across the same Poor Soul twice before. He had been given to understand that life was something of a one-way process, and wherever it exited, it was not meant to be here.

"Yes," The Soul continued, clearly uncomfortable but resolved to get through the encounter nonetheless, "I thought perhaps you might. Um. It was a rather nice little European number? About so long? Ended with a death at sea."

"Ah, yes, I remember now," admitted Quince, deciding that this one was not going to be fobbed off, and might as well be tackled head-on, "How did you like it?"

"Well, the sea was nice," said the Soul quickly, obviously eager not to hurt Quince's feelings, "But, well, it wasn't exactly what I'd had in mind..."

"Really? You must have liked the death, at least?"

"Actually, I didn't get to that bit," the Soul confessed, somewhat sheepishly.

"Didn't get to it!" exclaimed Quince, thunderstruck, "Well then, however did you get here?"

"Oh, you know..." said the Soul vaguely.

"I'm afraid I don't"

"Well, it was simple, really," stammered the Soul, "I just, well, *decided* that it wasn't really my cup of tea. You know, it was very comfortable and all that but it just didn't feel, well, *me*."

"You just *decided* to come back?" said Quince, disbelievingly. He had never thought that this might be even remotely possible.

"Yes." Said the Soul, and then plunged on quickly before its courage could fail, "The thing is, you see, I kept finding myself thinking about that *other* life."

"Other life," interrupted Quince sharply.

"Yes, you know, that one you were looking at when I first came to see you."

"Don't know what your talking about," growled Quince through metaphysical teeth which were, metaphysically, gritted.

"Oh, surely you remember? You were looking at it quite closely when I arrived. Well, there was just something about that life which sort of *glowed* at me. I'm afraid I don't know how else to put it..." The Soul trailed off apologetically.

There was an extended silence.

Quince was just wondering how he might go about getting rid of the Soul when the little thing piped up suddenly.

"Oh, here it is," it exclaimed happily, "Yes, this is the one I'm talking about."

To Quince's horror, he suddenly found that the Soul had somehow managed to locate the life – the *familiar* life, *his* life! – and had drawn it close.

"Excuse me! Excuse me!" he shouted wildly, and pulled the life back away from the Soul. "Sorry," he went on, sounding not a bit of it, "These things aren't to be touched by anyone but the Management. Company policy," he added belatedly.

"Oh, yes, of course," said the Soul quickly, "I quite understand. Only, I thought that well, if the Soul who reserved it hasn't turned up, well then, I might as well have it...?"

Quince took the life quickly, and hid it behind him. He decided abruptly that this had gone on long enough. Why should he, the special man, the Gatekeeper, the Big Deal, why should he be made to feel wretched by a mere Poor Soul? It was ridiculous! No, he must end this now.

"I quite understand your concern, Sir," he began with polite firmness, "But it's out of my hands, see? We operate a strict no-returns policy, I'm afraid. Myself, well, I'd love to let you have this life, but it's not up to me, is it? No, so if you'd like to go back to the life you left down there, then I'm sure you can bring up the matter with the appropriate authorities when you get to the Other Side..."

Quince trailed off.

He realised suddenly that the Soul had taken on a strange, almost glazed over appearance. It was not hearing what he was saying anymore. In fact, he was not even sure it was looking at him at all. It was almost as if it was looking *through* him...

Quince shifted a moment too late.

As has been said, there was no space here.

Nevertheless, there were different places that one could decide not to occupy space in, and the Soul had abruptly decided that it wanted not to occupy the same non-space as Quince.

The impact hurt quite a lot for something that had absolutely no mass.

As they fell together, Quince turned. He was aware of the life he had been hiding behind him. It was very near, and Quince had time to think that it seemed much larger and more real than it had ever seemed to him before.

Then they hit it.

For a moment they formed a frozen tableau. Quince, the familiar life, and the Poor Soul all merged together in the diaphanous, hallucinatory way of things caught in the interstitial spaces either side of reality.

Then they all vanished into an infinitely thin sliver of void which bubbled away silently into the ether.

There was warmth here and comfort, and Quince had a vague notion that he was not alone, that the Poor Soul was with him, and he held onto the awareness of this and an awareness of who he was for a little while before it leeched away from him like a dream on waking, and he became firmly and finally embroiled in the *now*, which was of course constantly changing, shrinking around him then emptying outwards, becoming cold and hostile, and lungs he had now, little lungs filling with cold fresh air, filling, screaming, pumping, he writhed on huge hands that held him gently, soothing him, and was moved to breast and Mother-Protection, a sanctuary which was his for an age until he grew bold and moved away on little legs growing ever stronger, taking him on his own wild adventures through early childhood, when, with shocking violence, he was taken away from those who loved him by an accident and placed in an orphanage, there to grow with blemishes and scars into adolescence, clever and suffused with talents but also wreathed in pain, and leaving here as soon as he could he leapt into life with abandon and passed through many strange and wonderful and terrible things until the fire cooled a little and love took him for the first time and carried him reeling against the harsher currents but with purpose until he begat and begat and begat a third and final time whence love was ripped from him once more, and he found

solace in his middle years in his children until they too left, and he was

once more alone but for a few friends who touched his surface as he

touched theirs, in a vague, removed way, but which nevertheless helped

and made some times joyous and others simply bearable, (and coming

towards him suddenly were the shoes, the trainers, laced with gold, looking

so strangely familiar that he suddenly wondered if there was perhaps a

God or at any rate a god, something more than he had ever thought

possible, so strong and strange was the feeling of recognition at the

moment when he found them, but then they too receded into the past

along with the rest of his spent life and were gone and the feeling of

connection passed), but these friends gradually moved away, or passed

away, or found others to whom their souls passed in favour of him, and he

reached a point when his hair was silver when he realised his whole life

was characterised by loneliness and loss, and so devoted his remaining

years to pouring over old books which described strange rituals and

heathen rites, in the hope that he might find some crack in reality into

which he could fit a lever and thus prise for himself a piece of creation that

he could form around his existence to make himself more attractive to

others, and in so doing secure their love for always and ever, so that he

might never be alone again; and finding such spells in obscure abundance,

he indulged in them fanatically, and sometimes felt as if they were almost

working, and sometimes felt as if there was something else within him, a

half-remembered presence of *other*, and this gave him the hope he needed

to pursue his endeavours with renewed vigour, until, finally he died whilst

in the midst of one such ritual, old and desiccated, the unintended victim of an arcane rite of frightfully complex, vaguely hopeful, and magnificently erroneous conceit.

He tumbled out of the other end of the life, into a bright white place. Picking himself up, he yawned, stretched, and looked around, wondering vaguely what he was supposed to do next. He could not remember quite why he was meant to be here. Then again, he could not quite remember who he was, or where *here* was in the first place, so he decided not to worry about it too much for the moment.

After a while, he realised he was not alone. A little way off, there was a line of other people. They seemed similarly bemused in a benign, un-worried sort of a way, so he decided to go and join them.

"Hello," he said genially to the person ahead of him, joining the back of the queue.

"Hello," said the person ahead of him, smiling a little.

"Excuse me, but do you know what we're queuing for?" he asked, at length.

The person ahead of him thought for a while. The line shuffled forward.

"Haven't the foggiest, I'm afraid," the person said at length.

The person ahead of him seemed faintly worried about this for a moment, but then he shrugged, "But I suppose it'll all become clear in a moment," they went on, brightening up.

He shrugged too. This seemed reasonable.

Eventually, he got near to the head of the queue.

There was a large benign looking being there, handing out tickets.

The person ahead of him was given a ticket, looked rather happy, and promptly vanished through a big white door into nothing.

Then it was his turn. He held his hand out for a ticket. The being leant forward as if to give him one, then checked himself.

The being looked him up and down carefully.

"'ang on a minute," the being said slowly, "What's goin' on 'ere then?"

"Sorry?" he replied, quite unsure what the problem was.

"Well, there's two of you in there, in't there!" exclaimed the being.

"What?" he replied, confused, "Is there?"

"Yes!"

"Oh, well, I'm terribly sorry. I don't want to be any trouble, you know." he really felt quite contrite.

"Most irregular, that, most irregular," said the being severely, looking rather troubled, "Gonna throw the whole system out of whack, that is, if I let you through."

"Oh, well I wouldn't want to be the cause of any problem," he said, "Would it be better if I just go back?"

"Ooo, you can't do that!" said the being, sounding scandalised, "Nah, it's a one-way thing, innit? No going back, mate, sorry."

"What should I do then?" he asked.

"You'll just 'ave to wait here, I suppose."

"Ah," he said, and moved aside to let the others in the queue past.

After a rather large amount of non-time he had an idea.

"Look, as long as I'm here, is there anything I can do to help?" he asked brightly.

The being considered this thought for a minute.

"Well, the thing is, see, I can't let you any further on, on account of there's somehow more 'n one of you in there," the being was speaking slowly, considering each word carefully.

He nodded sagely, as if he understood.

"And just out of interest, what is further on?" he asked politely.

"Why, Level Two, of course!" said the being, "What you've been training for, back there in Level One. Oh, it's a whole new ball game in there mate, believe me!"

He frowned for a moment. He hadn't considered there had been anything previous to this big white land, but now that he thought about it, he *did* seem to remember there being something before.... "Shoes," he thought to himself, "Shoes with a nice gold stripe. I wonder what shoes are?" For some reason, this thought bothered him a little. But he decided to let it go. After all, he had enough to worry about at the moment.

"But I can't go on to Level Two, though?" he asked, just to clear things up.

Jamie Brindle

"No, mate, 'course you can't!" the being said, "It'd be an unfair advantage, wouldn't it? With two of you in there, and all!"

"Ah, I see. And I can't go back to Level One, either. So, is there anywhere else I could go where I could be of service?" he asked.

The being considered this.

"We-ell," it said, slowly, "I do hear they're rather understaffed back at the Beginning."

"The Beginning?"

"Yeah, you know, where it all starts? I hear it's a real shocker of a mess down there. It's a bit outside the rules, but if you fancy it, maybe you could go back there and help out. Tidy things up a bit, sort of thing?"

He thought about it for a moment. It seemed reasonable.

"Alright," he said, nodding, "If you think it would help."

"Oh, it'd help alright!" the being said, "No question there! It'd help everyone! You'd be lending a hand where it's wanted, and well, between you and me The Beginning's the best bit anyway! So probably good for you too, mate, actually."

"So we have a deal then?" he asked happily, holding out his hand.

The being considered for a moment, then shook warmly.

"Yes mate!" the being said, "We've got ourselves a big deal!"

The being snapped it's large fingers. Abruptly, he felt the world begin to stream away backwards. Everything became faint.

But before it was lost entirely, the being called out to him.

"Now, remember there's no memory back at The Beginning!" it was saying, "On account of there being no time! Don't worry, in time it'll all make sense! Oh and here, take this back with you". The being hurled something at him. He caught it. "That's the life you rode in on, mate. Might as well find some use for it! I'm sure some Poor Soul will want it..."

And with that, the voice trailed away and was lost.

Quince stood, surveying his domain with satisfaction. For a moment, he felt a little odd, as if something was slightly out of phase with how things should be. He frowned to himself. He felt slightly...full. As if he had more substance than he should have. For a moment, he almost fancied he heard a strange – yet strangely familiar –voice echoing in his head. He puzzled at the feeling for a moment, but could not quite grasp it, and so let it go. It faded away like a dream.

He looked down. Ah yes. He was holding a life in his hands. How did this one end, he wondered? For some reason, he felt as if this life was important, somehow. It was as if it were tugging on him. He wondered why that might be. What could any one life contain that would make it more attractive to him than any other life?

He was just about to skim through it in an attempt to find out, when he noticed a client had arrived. He smiled brightly. He did love his job.

Putting the life to one side amid an infinite pile of other lives, he turned to face the Poor Soul.

"So," he began cheerily, "What can I do for you?"

Jamie Brindle

"Oh, I'd like a life please," breathed the Poor Soul.

"Would you, now?" grinned Quince, grabbing a life from the pile, "Well, this is a most agreeable life, it ends quite spectacularly..."

"The thing is," the Poor Soul interrupted him, "What was that life you were holding when I arrived...?"

The End

Jamie Brindle

Skeleton Jack

Skeleton Jack dances under the full moon, and all the girls dance with him.

Out they come, from the huts and from the fields, against their better judgment and despite their parents' pleadings.

"Don't go a-dancing with Jack!" warn their mothers, "He dances to one tune, and no good can come of it!"

But Jack's hips are limber and his bright eyes are cruel.

"Don't dance with Jack," say their fathers, "His feet are fleet, and he'll dance you all away!"

But Jack's slippery shape is alabaster beauty in the slanting moonlight, and all the girls do swoon.

So Skeleton Jack makes his dance, right there outside the village in the dusty ground, and not a man with mans-blood in his veins can come out to challenge him, for that is his magic, on this night which is his alone.

Now out comes Daisy, and all around would agree that Daisy is the fairest, the straightest-standing, so tall, so slender, so fresh and tender. Out she comes to dance with Jack, and the world holds its breath.

Jack takes her hand and spins her in the moonlight, and the plumes of dust look like dark blood at their feet.

Skeleton Jack, he is the very devil. He is handsome as a devil, too, for all his gauntness, for his movements pulse like life itself, and he is dressed in silken finery.

"Oh come back, girl, come back in!" calls her father, pressed up against the window of his cottage, and able to come no closer, "Jack is a stranger, and he'll make a stranger of you!"

But the roar of blood is in her ears, and Daisy does not hear.

Before long, the moon begins to fade; but Jack has made his choice, and his night is nearly done.

Away he dances, and all around him drop the girls, like puppets with slit strings, down to the ground and down into sleep, deep, deep, deep, cold and silent and still.

Away he dances, and dances Daisy with him.

When the sun comes up, Daisy's father can come out; but his girl is long away.

Skeleton Jack returns to his cave of brightly glittering carvings, and Daisy is in a swoon.

There are many fine things here, oh so many fine and glittering things; and each one was once a girl, just like Daisy. Now they are merely things; oh, but aren't they pretty?

Jack leads Daisy to a place by the fire and lays her gently down. He gets out his cooking pot and all his special herbs. And now he makes a soup.

Daisy smells the simmering pot, and stirs up from her sleep.

She looks around, all wide of eye, and wonders where she is.

Skeleton Jack reaches a long hand out into the darkness under the earth and snaps the neck of a deep-burrowing mole. He pulls it back and smiles at her and starts squeezing it into the soup.

"My dear, my lovely," he whispers to her, "Tell me, what is your true name?"

But Daisy, who is sometimes wise, shakes her head and replies, "I'll not give you that for free!" and shivers in the darkness.

Jack is patient. He has played this game for many long years.

He shades his bright eyes and runs his nails through the mud, skewering seventeen fat ripe worms and stirring them into his soup.

"My dear, my lovely," he cajoles her, "Tell me, what price is your true name?"

And Daisy, who is sometimes brave, runs her slender hands down her tender thighs and replies, "The price of my name is that song you sing, the one that makes us dance!" and she licks her lips in the darkness.

Jack is slow to anger, despite the girl's pride. He needs her true name; the dance alone won't do, and neither will the soup.

So he scuttles away to a corner where a pool of putrid water festers, and fishes out a stinking fish, white of eye in the darkened cave, and lobs it into the soup.

"My dear, my lovely," he purrs to her, "*This* is the song I sing, though no one can sing it like me!"

And with that he sings the song for her, which no one before has remembered, because on Jack's night when the moon is full, all the important things are forgotten.

And Daisy listens to the song, and locks it into her mind, and remembers it very closely.

"There, my dear, my lovely," says Skeleton Jack, and his eyes are burning cold, "Now you have heard my song. Will you not let me have your one true name?"

And Daisy, who will sometimes risk great things on narrow chances, bites her full red lip until the blood runs, and replies, "My true name is Skeleton Jack, and this is *my* cave, and that is *my* broth, and you are *mine alone*!"

Oh, how Jack does wail!

Up jumps Daisy – and singing Jack's song, she dances Jack's dance; and what can Jack do but dance too?

Daisy writhes and sways; and Jack is hers indeed.

She picks up the broth and spits into it, once, twice, and again; and now her blood is mixed in, and the broth is hers indeed.

Then, "Drink!" she commands, and of course he does; how can he do otherwise?

Jack shakes, and he howls, and he cries, and he pleads.

But Daisy, she is very cold.

Jack shrinks as he shakes, and glows as he howls.

But Daisy, she has made her choice.

Jack is gone: in his place, a brightly gleaming carving, beautiful and thin.

And Daisy, she is Daisy no more.

Skeleton Jack is gone from these parts, though his story is told in the hills.

Daisy never came back; and her father, he sickened and died.

But not long after she went away, many lost girls came home. They tumbled and fumbled back from the earth, covered in mud and mildew, and not a day older than when Jack had danced them away. Some were welcomed by fathers still living. Others came home to find a hundred years had slipped by.

Now the mothers look to their sons, for Skeleton Jack had his dance stolen, and the woman who whispers the young men out into the moonlight is very thin and very beautiful, and no one has said, 'no' to her yet.

The End

Jamie Brindle

I Want To Believe

General Xan Tuleep, First Speaker for the Empire of Darkstar, and also religious leader aboard the ship, wiped the foam of delicious plasma from his fourteen moist lips and turned to address Captain Funnelsqueak.

"Dead? What do you mean, dead?" General Xan furrowed both layers of eyes and used his tail to clean the wax out of his single huge abdominal ear.

"Yes, dead, I'm afraid," said Captain Funnelsqueak apologetically, "It seems these creatures are a particularly hard breed of nut to crack. Not one of them so much as gave even name, rank, or number, not even under the most exquisite forms of torture we have at our disposal. They simply endure; then they die."

General Xan growled deep in his underthroat.

"Blast it!" he exclaimed, "Well then, there's nothing for it: we'll have to get another one of the buggers."

Captain Funnelsqueak bowed.

"Of course, sir," he acquiesced, "I have taken the liberty already of determining suitable coordinates. I have located what seems to be a promising indigene. All that we require is your word, and we shall jaunt out of low orbit and obtain the subject directly."

General Xan nodded his upper head in assent, signalled the audience was at an end with a casual flick of his tail, and idly regurgitated the solid portion of his recent meal back into his first three stomachs.

Captain Funnelsqueak bowed once more and took his leave.

"And Captain," General Xan called after his departing minion, "No more mistakes. Darkstar is ready for the invasion. All we require are the coordinates of their secret base, and their world will be ours for the taking..."

General Xan cackled to himself, shook his golden mane manfully, and with a vain glance in the mirror, straightened a few of his more unruly antennae.

In his attic bedroom, surrounded on three sides by walls crowded with pictures and postcards and newspaper cuttings, Matthew ate the plate of food his mother had kept warm for him and continued composing his letter to *UFOlogy UK* magazine.

He had been working on the letter for most of the evening. He was rather proud of it. The letter was addressed to the editor, but the main body of the work (which took up 17 pages so far) was concerned with enumerating the many errors and misconceptions contained within a letter that had appeared in the previous issue of *UFOlogy UK* magazine. The letter had been authored by Philip Frogmore, who was acknowledged as an expert in the field, which rather rankled with Mathew, who acknowledged

Jamie Brindle

the man as nothing more than a rather tall species of buffoon. Mathew regularly ran into Mr Frogmore on the convention circuit, and had enjoyed a rather spirited enmity with him ever since it had become obvious (to Matthew) that the older man had been stealing his ideas from an Internet chat room they both frequented. Mathew wouldn't have minded so much, only the ideas had proven wildly popular with other UFO enthusiasts, and had resulted in Mr Frogmore gaining a sort of golden cache within the community.

The light slanting in through the large attic window that occupied most of one wall had begun to fade, but Mathew had been so absorbed in his work that he had hardly noticed.

He frowned, crossed out the word "flawed", replaced it with the word "moronic", and completely failed to notice Moses snuffling under his fingers and absconding with half a sausage.

He yawned and squinted in the darkness. This was taking longer than he had anticipated.

He put the end of the pencil in his mouth, placed a chip firmly behind his ear, and got up to turn the light on.

His hand was just about to touch the switch, when a strange humming noise began to permeate the room. It started very softly, a subtle shifting, buzzing sound that seemed to come from everywhere and nowhere, from behind the walls, even from within Mathew himself.

He stopped and cocked his head to one side.

As suddenly as it had begun, the noise subsided.

"Squeak," said Moses, poking his nose out guiltily from behind a pile of cushions. His fat little cheeks were stuffed full of sausage, and his whiskers quivered, testing the air carefully.

"Did you hear that too, Moses?" asked Mathew.

"Squeak," replied Moses, which is pretty much the extent of a hamster's vocabulary.

"What do you think it was?"

"Squeak," said Moses thoughtfully, before scuttling up onto the bedpost and flinging himself with suicidal gusto off into space and towards his master's outstretched hand.

Mathew caught the little ball of fur as it blurred through the air. He gave Moses an idle stroke, and listened again for the noise.

There was nothing now.

Just the beating of his heart.

Just the distant gusting of the wind outside.

Just silence.

A beam of intense green light shot in through the window. The entire room was bathed in a strange, otherworldly luminescence, picking out the posters and pictures pasted to the walls.

I WANT TO BELIEVE, screamed a tatty poster in the reflected bilious light that was shouldering its way into the room.

Outside the window, a humming, spinning disk of boiling illumination rotated in the darkness.

Mathew gaped.

"Oh," he said.

The shape outside the window loomed closer.

It was huge.

As Mathew stared on, a tubular structure folded out of the shining smoothness of the ship's hull. It prodded experimentally at the window, seemed satisfied with the diagnosis of "glass" and pulled back.

Then it rammed the window.

There was a shattering noise, and all at once wind seemed to own the whole world.

It was roaring in past the broken shards of glass, rustling the papers on the desk, sucking up the unfinished plate of food, tussling the bed sheets and pulling at Mathew's clothes.

Surely the weather outside wasn't as windy as this?

Then the wind was clawing at Mathew's hair, ruffling his shirt collar and ballooning the bottoms out of his flared trousers.

It was a funny thing, reflected the calm part of Mathew's mind. You waited your whole life to be abducted by aliens, you researched the topic exhaustively, you actually attempted to contact UFO's directly by means of amateur radio, trance-like meditation, and even (during a time of particularly intense paranoia) via a personal advert in the local newspaper's dating section. But when it actually came to it, being abducted by aliens was rather a frightening experience, and one that Mathew decided he would rather avoid, if at all possible.

Battling against the raging wind, Mathew turned around and made for the door.

He placed one hand on the handle.

"Squeaaaaak," said Moses, forlornly.

With a small slurping noise, the little hamster was sucked out of Mathew's hand.

He whipped around, just in time to see the ball of fur zoom across the room towards the window.

And into the mouth of the tube that was protruding in from the spaceship outside.

Mathew suddenly realised.

The tube wasn't just a tube.

It was a giant vacuum cleaner.

And it had just sucked Moses away.

For a moment, Mathew wavered, torn between the loyalty he felt towards his hamster (of whom he was very fond) and an intense desire not to recast himself in the grand opera of life as a human piece of dirt.

A last, morose, "Squeak," echoed back out of the tube.

Mathew locked eyes with the beautiful woman depicted numerous times on posters around the room.

"I...WANT...TO...BELIEVE!" he shouted, and threw himself towards the sucking tube.

There was a loud popping noise.

Everything went black.

Captain Funnelsqueak rubbed his talons together nervously and signalled for permission to enter the recreational bathing suite.

There was a haughty pause before the bioware computer that controlled the whole ship bleeped briskly and slid the door open, engulfing him in a plume of boiling green steam.

"Funnelsqueak?" boomed the voice of General Xan, "Is that you?"

Captain Funnelsqueak ducked to allow his ridged spine entry beneath the low doorway and made his oblations before his superior.

"Yes, my lord," confirmed Funnelsqueak, "I am sorry to interrupt your ablutions, but I came to tell you that we have obtained a new captive from the doomed planet."

Funnelsqueak moved forward and the steam thinned a little, to reveal the vast glistening bulk of General Xan, and the three small votaries that darted around him, cleaning his nooks with small wire brushes.

"Ah, excellent work, Funnelsqueak!" exclaimed General Xan, "All go smoothly, did it?"

Captain Funnelsqueak opened his gills to allow the delicious rot-scented steam in and nodded to the affirmative.

"Yes indeed, my lord," he said brightly, "Our cloaking device is still holding up admirably against the native's attempts to break it, and though they are no doubt aware that we are here in a general sense, they have no clue as to our current location, and could not have hoped to intercept us during our brief jaunt down to the planet's surface."

General Xan gurgled and eyed the votary that was cleaning between his lateral noses with hunger.

"Good, good," he said, "And this subject is high up in their command, is he?"

Captain Funnelsqueak smiled broadly.

"Oh, yes, sir," he replied, "Our intelligence reports that the subject is a member of the elite ranks of those who rule this puny planet. He will know the location of the base, for certain,"

"Marvellous," muttered General Xan, before opening his mouth and signalling impatiently for the votary to get inside. Thrilled at the honour, the small creature gave a shrill shriek of delight at the prospect of being assimilated, made a small obeisance to the gods, and leapt into the gaping maw.

There was a steady crunching noise.

General Xan burped loudly.

"Urgh!" he spat, his face folding in on itself in disgust, "That votary had some quite unholy thoughts! I must obtain more devout servants in the future..."

"Um, there was *one* thing," Funnelsqueak began nervously, "It seems that we inadvertently obtained the subject's pet, as well as the subject himself."

General Xan mulled the thought over.

"Is it dangerous?" he asked at length.

"Oh, no! Not at all!" Funnelsqueak replied hastily, "Quite a stupid, peaceful species. I understand that they are quite popular pets with the members of the elite of this world. Something of a status symbol."

General Xan did some more mulling. He rather enjoyed a good mull.

"Not to worry, Captain," he pronounced at length, "And if he really is that fond of his pet, perhaps the blasted thing will give us some more leverage with the subject. Now," he went on, heaving himself out of the boiling, putrid pool and carelessly crushing one of the two remaining votaries beneath his hoof, "Since time is such a pressing matter in this regard, let us not waste any! We must interrogate the prisoner directly!"

Captain Funnelsqueak nodded his antlers enthusiastically, and backed out of the bathing suite.

"Now, it seems to me that the best form of torture for something like this..." said General Xan, his voice fading to silence as he and the Captain made their way to meet the prisoner.

Alone, rejected, denied the great honour enjoyed by its sisters, the last remaining votary knelt in the steaming, bubbling pool of sloughed filth and tried to console itself with a long, soothing drink.

The darkness was so complete that at first Mathew thought he was dead. His body felt strange and light, and his head seemed clouded, as if someone had pumped smoke in through his ears and short-circuited his brain.

Where am I? He thought.

The events immediately preceding his arrival here in the darkness seemed rather confused. He remembered eating his dinner...and he was writing a letter to someone...then there was a strange sound...and then...

All at once, he recalled the huge, glowing shape outside his window, and the questing vacuum cleaner that had sucked him away...

He had been abducted.

He tried to stand up, an act which was hampered considerably by the fact that he was hanging upside down by a rope tied to his feet.

The rope bit into his ankles, and he yelped.

Well, it didn't seem as if he would be walking around any time soon...

Instead he tried looking around. This attempt was, essentially, no more effective than the first, given the almost complete lack of light in...well, in whatever sort of room it was that he was hanging upside down in.

The room was totally dark.

Although...

Actually, it seemed a little more greyish than it had done a minute before.

He fancied he could just make out the edges of surfaces, faint traces in the blackness.

He opened his eyes as wide as he could.

Yes, the room was definitely getting lighter.

He could just about make out his hand when he flapped it in front of his face. He looked up towards his feet. The rope wrapped around his ankles and glinted in the twilight. He could see where it joined the ceiling, maybe ten feet above his, well, feet.

Something glinted brightly in the corner of his vision. He swung his body around in time to see earthrise through the large porthole window that took up a huge chunk of the room.

It was magnificent.

Sunlight glinted on the Atlantic, slanting down through iridescent patches of white cloud, sparkling off the yellow sands of Africa and blotting out the stars in half the sky. He could see the wave of nighttime that still engulfed half of Europe, could see a thousand pinpricks of light glittering up from the cities filled with the teeming millions of pulsing humanity.

"My days..." breathed Matt.

"Squeak," agreed a familiar voice from behind him.

Matt whipped around. The room was fully illuminated now, bathed in the reflected luminescence of Earth.

Moses was only a few feet away from him. He hadn't noticed him in the darkness.

The small hamster hung by his own, much thinner, length of rope from the ceiling. His forepaws were tied together, too.

"Squeak," he said again, his nose twitching earnestly.

Matthew reached out a hand. Strain as he might, he could not quite reach Moses.

He began rocking his body back and forth, trying to build up a momentum that would carry him within grasping range of his beloved little pet.

There was a cold, grinding noise.

A door opened in the wall opposite the porthole. Suddenly, a new light was streaming into the room, bright and clinical.

And with the light came the aliens.

Mathew considered himself fairly well versed in the various types of extraterrestrials that other enthusiasts had catalogued and categorized over the years. Some were small and thin, with big heads and grey skins. Some were tall and broad, with tails and forked tongues. Some looked rather like human beings with Cornish pasties glued to their foreheads.

But none of them looked like the two ghastly creatures that were even now rolling in through the door towards him.

They were enormous and slimy and scaled. They had eyes where there should be noses and buttocks where there should be mouths. They had at least seven appendages that Mathew could not even name.

And they smelt awful.

Mathew tried to scream, but all that came out was a twisted little, "Pth," sound.

They loomed towards him.

They reached out horrible sharp talons to rend him...

They ignored him entirely.

"So, my pretty," gloated General Xan, reaching out his three primary hands towards the alien leader, "It seems that you are in quite a pickle, aren't you?"

"Squeak," said Moses, firmly.

"Yes, yes, I believe that's what your comrades said, too," General Xan gave an ugly laugh, "They said that right up to the end. It took rather a long time though, didn't it Captain Funnelsqueak?"

"Oh, indeed my lord," agreed the Captain, "Quite an excruciatingly long time. They begged us to stop, in the end."

"Squeak?" said Moses, the first trace of doubt entering his voice.

"Stop? Of course we didn't stop!" replied General Xan, who had grown so excited by all this ghastliness that his stink gland had started to boil,

"Oh no, we didn't stop for them, and we won't stop for you...unless, of course, you would care to tell us the location of your secret base?"

Moses twitched his whiskers uncertainly.

"Squeak," he said at length, narrowing his eyes.

"Very well," laughed General Xan, "It seems you give us no choice..."

He reached out towards the furry alien leader...

At the last moment he pivoted round on his central boneshaft and leered at the alien's pet.

"What a horrible little toy you have," General Xan declaimed, then, as an aside to Captain Funnelsqueak, "Is it sentient, do you think?"

Captain Funnelsqueak shook his head firmly to the negative.

"A salient point, my lord, but no," he said, "It is quite impossible that such an unfathomably ugly creature could attain anything but the most rudimentary trappings of awareness. For instance I am sure it can perceive pain..."

"Argh!" said Mathew.

"And pleasure..."

"Oooh!" said Mathew.

"But beyond that, it is quite a simple, harmless life form, I am sure," concluded Captain Funnelsqueak, removing his organic nerve stimulation appendage from the alien pet.

General Xan moved closer to get a better look.

"My, my, what a hideous thing…" he mused. He began poking randomly at parts of the strange creature.

"What is this, Funnelsqueak?" he demanded.

"Ah, I believe that is the life form's nose, sit," supplied the Captain.

"What, it only has the one?" General Xan was incredulous, "And what about this?"

"That, if I am not very much mistaken, is the creature's windpipe," said Captain Funnelsqueak, "You can tell by the rather pleasing shade of blue it's face is turning."

"I see," General Xan was nodding, "And what about…oh!"

Captain Funnelsqueak stared on in horror.

The terrible creature relaxed its iron grip on Mathew's throat, letting air back into his starved lungs.

He was trying to scream, but no sound would come.

He watched in horror as the monster reached up towards his trousers.

Something slipped out of his pocked, dislodged by the brushing of the hand.

It caught the light as it fell towards the floor.

It was half a chip.

He remembered now. He had accidentally put it behind his ear just before this whole abduction business had taken place. From there he had shoved it in his pocked just before being sucked up by the giant vacuum cleaner.

Now it was spinning down towards the ground.

It surprised General Xan as it fell past his lower nose, causing him to breath in sharply from the shock.

The chip was sucked into the General's gaping maw.

"Urgh!" said General Xan, "What the hell was that?"

But already his highly advanced digestive system had begun to work on the alien organic matter.

General Xan was a member of an extremely evolved species, battered into shape by countless millions of years of ruthless natural selection, and honed to utter sharpness by the very latest in intergalactic genetic engineering.

And owing to his role as ultimate religious leader aboard the ship, he had been designed with a few special features in mind.

High Priests – such as General Xan – were endowed with the ability of consuming their underlings and assimilating their thoughts, feelings, even nuances of character into their own being. This gave some sway with the devout underlings, who were very much reassured by the fact that, if they were given the honour of being consumed by their priest, the afterlife would be on the cards almost as quickly as the after dinner mints. Of course, the real reason why the ruling class had adopted this system was that it was very easy to become aware of an impending revolution when all one had to do to find out was eat one of the suspected conspirators.

On the other hand, none of the highly intelligent genetic engineers who had designed General Xan's germ line had considered the perspective of an average English potato, let alone how it felt about being turned into an oven chip and marinated in a chemical soup of tomato ketchup and vinegar, before being stuffed into some ingrate's pocket, abducted, and finally consumed by a strange and horrible organism from a distant world.

In short, the potato was pissed.

Deep in its unravelling genetic code, the potato was furious.

And it was conveying its anger and confusion to General Xan.

"Urgh! Argh! Phnggg!" screamed General Xan, writhing around in agony and smashing into the walls of the room.

"My lord!" shouted Captain Funnelsqueak, "What's wrong?"

"Spling!" explained General Xan desperately, "Knurg! Phlug! Jhlinget!"

But try as he might, his language centres had been irrevocably scrambled by the alien DNA. He closed his eyelids to try and clear his head, but his mind was abruptly filled with the taste of mud and the endless clay of potato fields.

Captain Funnelsqueak leapt upon his raving leader, trying to subdue him.

Unnoticed, forgotten, Mathew began slowly swinging his body back and forth.

After a few moments he had built up sufficient momentum.

He made a swing for Moses.

He missed.

He waited until he swung close again, and made another lunge.

This time he managed to grab the tiny ball of fur in one hand.

As quick as he could, he undid the little knots that bound the hamster tight.

"Squeak!" exclaimed Moses triumphantly: he was free!

Now it was Mathew's turn. In a blur of fur, Moses scampered up Mathew's legs and began gnawing at the rope that bound his feet.

There was an ominous creaking noise.

Suddenly, the rope gave way.

"Ow!" said Mathew, rubbing his head, "You could have warned me you were about to do that!"

"Squeak!" tutted Moses reproachfully, before dashing off across the floor and out through the open door.

Mathew gave one last glance at the pair of horrible alien forms writhing around on the floor.

"The Masher!" General Xan was howling, while Captain Funnelsqueak tried desperately to calm him, "Oh! How we must fear the dreaded Masher!"

Shaking his head in disbelief, Mathew ran out of the room, following in the footsteps of Moses.

The ship was a maze. There were hundreds of corridors and passageway, portholes and doorways and rooms filled with strange, ominous machinery and sickly luminescent computer consoles that looked as if they had been grown rather than built.

But somehow, Moses seemed to know what he was doing.

Mathew followed the hamster as he scampered down a corridor, before ducking into a recess just in time to avoid a patrol of horrible, slimy aliens.

Then they were off again.

At last, they reached a door that was closed to them. Something was written in a brutal-looking language above the doorway. Mathew couldn't read the words of course, but he got the distinct impression that the message was a threatening one.

He hesitated.

But Moses scampered up towards the door and leapt from one recess to another, higher and higher, until he was standing on the level of a sort of hand pad, though the sort of hand that must fit a pad like that would be exactly the sort of hand the owner of which one would not like to meet on a dark night.

Moses nuzzled the pad with his nose.

There was an unhappy beeping noise.

A red light lit up above the door.

"Oh dear," said Mathew.

But Moses simply coughed.

WIth a wet little chewing noise, the remains of half a sausage were brought forth from his podgy cheeks.

The semi digested food fell into the bio-sampler of the computerised door.

The red light above the door began flashing urgently.

A siren started howling.

There was a broken hissing noise, and the door slid open in a plume of ominous black smoke.

"Squeak!" shouted Moses, and dashed inside.

Mathew followed.

Further in, there was another set of doors. These ones were open. Moses scampered through.

Mathew jumped in after the hamster, and the doors closed shut behind them.

They were in a small round room filled with computer equipment and keyboards. Lights flashed on and off efficiently. Through a small porthole, Matt could see the beloved blues and greens of Earth turning slowly in the void.

Moses poked at the controls with his nose.

There was a heavy thudding noise. The room seemed to shift under them.

Suddenly, the view out of the window was spinning, Earth rotating round and round, and alternating with a view of something huge and shining and ugly.

It took Mathew a moment to realise they had jettisoned out into space in some kind of escape pod.

But why is their ship on fire? Wondered Mathew.

It was true. Out in space, the mother ship was being torn apart by fires and explosions. It was spinning away from them and breaking up.

Inside their escape capsule, one small monitor showed a view from within the dying mothership.

"Don't fry me!" General Xan was wailing, "I don't want to be a potato chip!"

"Not the abattoir!" screeched the electronic voice of the ship's bioware mainframe, "I don't want to be a salami!"

"Squeak," coughed Moses, and nosed a button.

The screen went dark.

Mathew breathed a sigh of relief, as through the small porthole, beautiful Earth gradually swelled until it was the whole world.

Philip Frogmore stretched out one long, exquisitely manicured finger, and paused in the act of explaining why his theories about the connections between Atlantis and the Grey's were so groundbreaking.

The rapt crowd looked on. It was mainly made up of young women - an abnormality for a convention such as this – and Mr Frogmore was greatly enjoying the attention.

"So you see," he continued, "When the Grey's *left* Atlantis, not only did they know about the impending disaster, they had, in fact, actually *engineered* it..."

"What?" said a particularly pretty girl standing near the front of the crowd.

"I SAID," repeated Mr Frogmore, having to shout over the rising roar of noise that had just started up, and which was threatening to drown him out, "WHEN THE GREY'S LEFT..."

But at that moment there was a tremendous crash.

The world was cacophony.

Something came hurtling in through the roof of the convention centre. Stalls and counters and people were overturned and went flying.

Philip Frogmore was thrown from the podium and landed in a battered pile some meters away.

When he came to, he was amazed to see the strange object that had appeared on the stage. He looked up at the bright rays of sunlight that were slanting in through the staved-in roof. Dust and pieces of plaster were raining down on the crowd as they dashed up to the large object and began to investigate.

With a hissing noise, a hatch on top of the object popped open.

"Squeak!" said Moses.

"Oh, look – a hamster!" exclaimed the pretty young woman, "How adorable! Is there anyone else in there?"

Philip Frogmore gaped on in disbelief as the familiar face of his nemesis emerged from the alien escape pod.

"Hi everyone," said Mathew, clambering out of the pod, and sharing a smile with the particularly pretty young woman "Well, have I got a story to tell you all..."

Deep underground, in a secret location known only to the elite few who ruled the world and defended it ever and anon against the constant threat of alien invasion, Special Agent Ulfarious Sprinklenose III, AKA "Agent Moses", finished filing his report to his senior operative and relaxed back, enjoying the small crystal goblet of scented milk that was his one occasional vice.

There was silence for a long time.

"And your pet really has no idea about your true identity?" inquired the superior operative at length, "After all that he has seen, would it not be safer to liquefy him before he can compromise us?"

Agent Sprinklenose pondered the question, and ran one paw thoughtfully though his whiskers.

"No, I think we are safe on that score, at least," he pronounced after a moment, "He is more interested in the female he met when we landed than he is in the details of our little adventure."

"Good," said the superior operative, "I hope they behave themselves."

"And anyway," continued Agent Sprinklenose, "If he *did* decide to talk, who would believe him?"

The superior operative nodded sagely.

"He really thinks you are just another dumb animal?"

Agent Sprinklenose chuckled and shrugged his narrow shoulders.

"Squeak," he said.

The End

The Mesomorph

Well the Mesomorph he lives in a cave,

With blue bony fingers and hair in a braid,

And his heart is long broken,

And his words are well spoken,

And since he was born he was digging his grave.

Well the Mesomorph he is really quite ravaged,

By the thoughts that he thought he had locked in the attic,

And no one quite loves him,

And no one quite trusts him,

And no one remembers the boy who was savaged.

Well the Mesomorph he is old as the hills,

As the hills where he catches the game that he grills,

And he eats with great relish,

And he hopes he will perish,

And he hopes what he eats will forgive what he kills.

Well the Mesomorph he is broad and quite bitter,

Bitter with thoughts that burn as they glitter,

And remind him of losses,

And the burning of crosses,

And the land that he loved from that gilt Arab litter.

Well the Mesomorph he is flat in the face,

But he dresses in silks and diaphanous lace,

And these clothes are all soiled,

And thus beauty is foiled,

And all that results is a putrefied grace.

Well the Mesomorph he is gone away now,

Gone with a sigh and a moan and a growl,

And though his body is wasted,

And his mind madness tasted,

And his spirit disgraced id, we tip him a bow.

Organic Produce

Alice slips between the cracks, which is exactly how thin she wants to be.

One moment she is there, walking along the sidewalk, trailing reluctantly after her steamboat-broad mother through the autumn town, the next she is falling between the slits in the drain grating, and down she goes into the earth.

She is not scared, just silently overwhelmed that her plan has finally worked.

The other Alice – her favourite Alice – was handed her wonderland by a rabbit with poor timekeeping skills. But *this* Alice has had no such luck. That's why she has had to make herself so thin.

She plummets down, very far down, until the little patchwork of light above has vanished entirely, and now everything is full dark.

She falls right into her bed, and is horrified at the watered-down light seeping behind the curtains, at the unwelcome arrival of another day.

Alice often dreams about slipping under things or through things, about the world gaping wide and swallowing her whole. Sometimes she is on a small boat in a vast, furious ocean. Sometimes she falls down mineshafts or – most recently – between gratings. The horror never comes until she wakes up.

Alice dresses for work and goes downstairs.

Her mother has made her eggs and soldiers. The tops of the eggs have been sliced off and her mother stands behind her brushing her hair while she forces the soldiers down, sticky, slimy, moist balls that cling to her throat. She ignores the coffee, but washes down the food with half a glass of tepid tap water.

Her mother watches her get onto a bus, but is not there two stops later when Alice disembarks before she should, and walks into the public library. They have started to recognise her here, but Alice likes books anyway, and usually has the excuse of returning or borrowing one before using the toilet on the way out.

She wipes her mouth with the back of her hand and chews some gum.

Chewing gum is fine, as long as she spits the saliva into some tissue periodically, so long as she does not swallow.

She waits precisely three minutes for the next bus – she has the procedure very well planned – and this time gets off by the grocers, where she works.

Jamie Brindle

Alice watches the fruit turn. She likes this part of her job. She likes the still hours in the first half of the day, when the door opens only rarely and she hardly has to talk to anyone. She puts the fruit out early, and watches the skins shrivel and the flesh sag. Sometimes – but not so often that she thinks anyone is likely to notice – she forces one of her ragged nails through the skin of an apple, or snaps the neck of a banana. She feels triumphant as the hours pass, watching the imperfection spread through the ruined fruit, watching as a succession of customers inspect the fruit sadly, reject it, pass on. She likes to touch these pieces of fruit throughout the day, brush them with her hand, and think about what she has done to them.

Alice serves the silver-haired man, and he is waiting for her when it is time to lock up.

"What do you want?" she asks him.

"What do *you* want?" he replies.

She thinks about this all the way home while she eats the fruit she marked as her own earlier.

She gets home before her mother, and lets herself in with the key they used to leave under a broken paving slab for Toby. She has her own key, of course, but she always uses the one under the paving slab. During that simple sequence of actions – lift slab, scrape mud with fingers, remove cold metal, walk to door, turn key – during those simple actions, Alice is not Alice anymore, she is Toby.

She misses him.

This is the only thing that connects her to him anymore, these fifteen seconds every evening when she unlocks the door.

She sits in the darkness in the kitchen and tries to picture his face, but she doesn't think she can anymore. All she sees when she tries to see his face are photographs of his face, memories of memories, second hand and worn out.

Her mother comes home and Alice fixes them soup and bread.

After her mother goes to bed, Alice goes to the toilet. When she is done, she wipes her mouth, retrieves a small knife from a cabinet, and cuts a vein. She allows exactly thirty millilitres to drain into a beaker – ten for the soup, twenty for the bread – and flushes it down the toilet. She holds a wad of toilet paper to the cut until it stops bleeding, and flushes that away, too.

She goes to bed and dreams of a huge net of shadows, and her shadow being lost amongst them.

Alice serves the silver haired man again the next day, and again he is waiting for her when she locks up.

"Do you know what you want yet?" he asks her, and she nods.

"I want Toby back," she says.

"You didn't want him before," the man says reproachfully.

"I want Toby," she says again, looking fiercely at the tatty sleeves of the man's faded jumper.

He stares at her for the longest time, carefully, as if weighing something heavy against something strong.

Then he nods.

"Very good," he says, neutrally, but he gestures for her to cross the road with him.

They stand by the bus stop and examine their reflections in the shop windows opposite.

She shuts her eyes and he whispers something in her ear. When she opens them, he is standing by her other shoulder. The light has shifted, and Alice can't see her reflection anymore.

They wait for her bus, but when it arrives it is not her bus.

"Get in," says the man, and she does.

The bus takes them down a street that is not her street, and drops them at a house which is not her house.

Alice falters as they draw near to the back door. One of the windows is open – to let the hot, smoky smell of cooking escape into the clear night – and out through the window drifts the sound of a child singing.

She had forgotten how he sounds. Off-key, but so sweet.

How could she have forgotten his voice? Tears spring up in her eyes. She didn't think it was sweet, not before.

She bites her lip, and the man lays a gentle hand in the small of her back and pushes her on.

She walks up to the door, and of course it is open.

Alice walks inside.

Pots and pans simmer unattended. A chunk of roasting meat in the over is nearly ready.

The singing is coming from the lounge. Alice follows the childish voice.

She opens the door, and Toby is there, his small back to her, his blonde hair falling down his narrow neck. He is playing with a toy car and singing to himself for the fun of it.

She cannot see his face.

Her heart is hammering in her chest. She cannot see the silver-haired man, but she knows he is there, watching her.

She steps forward and lays a hand on her little boy's shoulder.

He turns.

His face is not his face.

It is her face, the face that she gave him.

The bite marks are livid; the lacerations where teeth have cut through flesh are ragged and ripped. One of his lips is missing, but he always had a lisp anyway.

She swallows, and that is a mistake, because she immediately remembers how it felt to swallow before, the last time that she had seen him, when her mother had cooked such a splendid meal, to celebrate their newfound freedom from annoying little commitments and annoying little voices.

She retches and heaves but nothing comes out except tears.

A small hand strokes her cheek gently, and her stomach stops its spasms. She kisses his warm hand, tasting the salt of his blood in the little ridges where the skin has been torn clean.

She wonders how her mother ever persuaded her that Toby's voice was not beautiful. It is *so* beautiful.

"Can I come home now, mummy?" he asks her.

Alice looks round at the silver-haired man, who nods his confirmation.

"Yes," she says, fervently, "Only, not like that."

The retching starts in her stomach again. This time she does not fight it.

The flesh comes back out, all his tender flesh. She laughs and cries blood and gently forces the wedges of tendon and muscle and smooth, smooth skin back into her boy, back where it should be.

Then she stands up and takes his hand.

They leave together, and the silver-haired man trails behind.

Alice walks back down the street that is not her street and takes the bus that is not her bus. All the way, Toby sings gently in her ear and they rock back and forth in time with the swaying of the vehicle. The silver-haired man sits just behind them. He does not say a thing.

By the time they reach the grocers again, the sun has set and the streets are deserted. Alice alights, and in the moment before her foot touches the asphalt she feels the world

S   T   R   E   T   C   H

back into place, and the silver-haired man is at her right shoulder and Toby is at her left, and their reflections are all shimmering brightly in the storefronts.

The silver haired man is looking at her, and there is not a hint of a smile to him.

"So you get what you want," he says, rolling the words slowly, pondering.

Alice nods. She understands what is coming next.

"But blood is heavy, and there must be balance," the silver haired man continues, reaching into a pocket and pulling out a peach.

He bites into the soft flesh, and dark juice rolls down his chin.

The wind blows, and the silver-haired man is gone.

There are no more buses, but Toby sings to them as they walk home.

Alice has them wait outside the house until all the lights go out, before unlocking the door and silently slipping inside.

They walk through the kitchen, and the silver moonlight glances off all the glittering knives in the knife rack, dances on the copper pans and the cheese-grater and the skewering forks.

Toby is still singing, but so quietly Alice can barely hear him.

They walk up the creaking stairs, but Alice knows which ones creak the worst, and she is very thin and light, anyway.

They stand outside her mother's bedroom. Alice can hear her heavy breaths rattling under the doorframe, and she turns the handle very gently.

Alice opens the door, and Toby follows her inside. She shuts the door behind her.

There is stillness, then a rattling, then stillness again.

Alice cooks all through the night, and Toby keeps her company. All the pots and pans are in use, and the oven is on full-blast. A certain smell begins to permeate the house, rich and sour at the same time. Alice opens the windows, and several of her neighbours stir uncomfortably in their sleep. Some wake up hungry.

The Bound Book

When dawn comes, she is nearly finished.

She spends over an hour packing what she has cooked into plastic boxes and biscuit tins, silver foil and recycled jam jars. Then she makes a call to a cab company.

The man gives her a strange look when he smells the air coming out of the house, but she looks at him coldly and he relents and helps her pack everything into the taxi. There are a lot of little packages, and the trunk is quite full.

He opens the front passenger door for her, but she wants to sit in the back, next to Toby.

Toby sings to her all the way to the grocery store; but there is something sad in his voice now, and Alice finds that she is crying.

The silver-haired man is waiting for her on the street corner. He is not smiling, but he looks satisfied as the cab driver helps Alice unload all the packages onto the pavement.

Alice unlocks the grocers and clears half of the aisles. Toby gently strokes her hair while she writes up a stack of signs that say things like, "HOME MADE PIE" and "ORGANIC GAMMON". She writes out a number of little price tags, and sticks them on her produce.

Customers begin to come in. Some of them buy fruit. Some of them buy other items. The silver-haired man smiles at all of these customers, and shakes them each by the hand.

It is nearly closing time when the police arrive, but most of the produce Alice has brought in has been sold by now.

They talk to her gently at first, but when it becomes clear that they want her to go with them, she breaks down and starts screaming, so they have to drag her out of the shop and force her into the car.

She stares desperately at Toby as he waves to her one last time, and boards a bus that is not her bus with the silver haired man, disappearing away into a place where the reflections are not right.

But when she stops crying she realises she can still hear him singing to her, very softly, and she is at peace because some small things, at least, now balance.

The End

The Other Option

"Yes, children, three of them," Quince concluded, leaning back slightly and smiling his winning smile, "But they die very quickly, and you do it on account of all the virgins you think you'll get your hands on once you get to heaven."

Quince was a salesman, although he never went door-to-door. He never had the need. All his clients came straight to him, because there was simply nowhere else to go.

"I see," breathed the Poor Soul, "I suppose that makes it quite acceptable,"

It frowned slightly.

"But tell me," It went on softly, "What is a virgin?"

Quince levered his smile up a notch.

"My friend," he enunciated warmly, "If you take this life, then that question will never bother you again."

Quince was a salesman, but he'd never so much as held a vacuum cleaner or driven a car. What he sold was much more precious.

What he sold was life itself.

He sat in his office – which was both infinitely huge and immeasurably small, on account of the fact that it existed in a place outside of both space and time – and dealt out lives to the Poor Souls, who came to him ever and again. Technically, his realm was not *quite* the beginning of existence – but it was so close that he almost fancied he could see it on a clear day.

The only beings he ever came across – as far back as he could remember, at least, which was very far indeed, if not quite forever – the only beings he ever saw were these Poor Souls, these clients of his. Essentially, they were lifeless shells, waiting to be filled with whatever life Quince took it into his head to offer them. There was never a lack, either of clients or of lives to give them.

Personally, Quince regarded existence as rather an obvious choice – a bit mainstream – and he was constantly surprised that his clients didn't look around more first and see what their other options were. But then, after all, why should he care?

As long as he had clients, that was all that mattered.

"No, I don't think *you* understand," said the scruffy-looking Soul, leaning back and regarding Quince with something that almost bordered on disdain, "I don't want that blasted life. I don't want *any* of your petty little lives, so just put them away and listen for a minute, won't you?"

Quince frowned darkly – he was unused to being addressed in such a tone – and woefully shook his head. But he liked to think of himself as a reasonable man – or at least, creature – so he put the life he had been offering the Soul away again, and cleared his throat wearily.

"And while we're at it, my name's not 'hey, you,' either, it's muttermutter,"

"What?" said Quince, who couldn't stand people who mumbled.

"I said, it's 'Soul Dog'," repeated Soul Dog, at least having the grace to look abashed.

There was a pregnant silence.

"I see," said Quince at length. He paused, "Go on then, what is it you want?"

The scruffy-looking Soul looked surprised for a moment, as if it were expecting a little bit more of a fight. It recovered quickly, however.

"Right, yes," it began hurriedly, "Well, you've been here quite a while, haven't you?"

"Yes," said Quince coldly, "Forever,"

"Of course, of course," stammered the Soul, "Which is exactly why we thought we'd come to you first. Let you know, sort of thing. It was only the polite thing to do, we thought."

Something in the Soul's tone made Quince wary. He nodded slowly.

"And?" he asked, interested despite himself.

"To let you know, I mean," The Soul looked a little embarrassed now, "And, well, to see if you wanted on board. To be honest, we could do with having someone with your experience on the team"

Quince leant back.

"What exactly is it you are doing?" he asked suspiciously.

"Oh, that's easy!" exclaimed the Soul, "We're going into business."

After Quince had finished shouting and the Soul had left – seeming even more dishevelled than when it had arrived – he felt he needed a little break to calm himself down and regain his composure. He moved away from the endless queue of Poor Souls and wandered around aimlessly in his ephemeral realm.

What nerve. What *nerve*!

To even *think* of setting up a rival business! He shook his head ruefully. The quality of Poor Souls was certainly on the decline, if this was the sort of riff-raff the system was throwing up these days.

He wondered briefly how the fellow had ever managed to scrape together enough of a personality to exhibit such wanton arrogance. You could tell just by looking at the scruffy Soul that he had never enjoyed the weight of a proper life. Probably the wretched thing had simply spent some non-time bumming around the pathetic little nooks and crannies which littered the void this side of existence. More than likely he would call the whole thing a "valuable learning experience" or other such nonsense, and use it as a pretext in an application for some minor clerical position on The Other Side.

Quince sighed heavily.

How he *hated* students.

After rather a lot of non-time had elapsed, Quince began to feel a little more like his usual self, and decided to make his way back to the heart of his realm and get on with the serious business of distributing the various shades of human triumph and misery which formed the ubiquitous colouring of every life he handled. But when he had made himself ready to receive his first client, he found to his horror that a most singular thing had happened.

Instead of the endless queue of clients stretching away into infinity, which usually formed the backdrop of his world, there was only one rather small, sad-looking Soul waiting for him.

The feeling of unease, which had been brought on by the visit of the scruffy looking Soul, and which he had only just managed to shake, retuned to him in full vigour.

Trying to stay calm, Quince hurriedly beckoned the Poor Soul over.

"Existence, pleas..." began the Poor Soul, but Quince cut him off.

"What is the meaning of this?" He demanded sharply.

The Poor Soul looked slightly hurt.

"But I thought we weren't allowed to ask that," the Soul wheedled, pointing to a sign that floated in the middle of nowhere above Quince's desk.

The sign read:

We thank you for not:

-Shoving

-Smoking

-Questioning the meaning of existence

Quince shook his head irritably.

"No, no, I didn't mean...." he rolled his eyes and spluttered incoherently, "I mean, well, where are all the others?"

"There aren't any," replied the Poor Soul, looking more pitiful than ever, "I'm the only one,"

"But there were *millions* of you here a moment ago," Quince was almost pleading now, "Where have they all gone?"

"They chose the other option," the Soul bobbed about a little and tried to look ingratiating, "I thought they were being silly," it added quickly, "I think your deal looks *much* better."

Quince – who could always be bought with flattery – found himself warming a little to the Poor Soul almost against his will, and calmed down somewhat.

"Well, it is, it is," he said more softly, "But...what could they possibly be offering that's more enticing than *life*?"

"Oblivion," said the Poor Soul simply.

"Oblivion?" ejaculated Quince, outraged.

"Yes, oblivion. Nothing. Nada. Void. Forever."

"And what on Earth is so appealing about that?" Quince was leaning very close to the Poor Soul now, staring desperately at it, willing it to answer him.

The Soul seemed to consider the question for a moment.

"We-ell," it said at length, "You don't have to get up quite as early, I suppose."

"What?!"

"You don't have to get up at all, in fact."

"And they all chose that over life?" Quince almost spat the question, "They could have had it all – excitement , adventure, fine wine, great sex, loss, and friendship, and ice cream, and love – they could have had had it all, and instead they chose...*not having to get up so early*?"

The Poor Soul shrugged.

"No one likes having to get up," it said.

Quince marched resolutely through the vast expanses of nothing that composed his realm, the Poor Soul tagging along forlornly behind him.

He'd show them! Oh, yes, they wouldn't get away with this, not when Quince was around!

Oblivion, indeed!

"I don't mean to be a nuisance," the Poor Soul said at length, "But would you mind telling me where we're going?"

"To stop this nonsense," replied Quince, grimly, "We're going to find the competition and make it very clear to them that they are simply *not wanted*. I mean, after all, how popular can oblivion actually...oh!"

At that moment they topped one of the strange crests of non-space, and Quince fell silent at the sight before him.

Stretching away into the deep distance they streamed, millions and millions and millions of them: Poor Souls, shuffling and silent and empty, floating from the blinding, unassailable light of the Beginning towards... what?

He could not make out where they were heading at first. Quince squinted; then he frowned; then he snarled – his quarry had been found.

He plunged into the queuing souls, bumping them aside with scientifically executed ill-humour, and made his way to the Establishment of his rivals.

"Excuse me, *if* you don't mind, thank you so very much," he muttered as he shoved the souls out of his way.

Floating in the nothingness, there it stood: a cheap, chipped desk, in front of a panel of three battered-looking chairs; behind the chairs, a wall hung silently, it's sole reason for existence apparently to provide a place for the posters to go. Quince did not recognise the posters, though they looked vaguely familiar and filled him with a sense of instinctive contempt. The first showed a green leaf from a plant that some of the people involved in Life seemed to find quite symbolic of some thing or another; it certainly seemed to be something that many people thought quite important. The second showed nine pictures of the same bearded and behatted man, identical except that each image was reproduced in a different horribly garish colour. The final poster showed an idiotic looking fat yellow man clutching an item Quince vaguely recognised as being something sweet and decidedly bad for you. He loathed all three of them on sight; but not so much as he instantly loathed the three souls seated on the chairs behind the desk.

One was sucking on a nasty-looking little hand rolled cigarette. Another was sporting a pair of designer jeans ostentatiously complemented with designer tears. But it was the third soul that caught Quince's attention. It was wearing a fluffy little beanie hat (Quince found it intrinsically annoying, and would have done so were he not already thoroughly annoyed with its wearer anyway) and a ridiculous pair of cheap plastic sunglasses. It was the soul who had pestered him earlier about the setting up of this rival business. It was Soul Dog.

Even as he watched, Quince saw Soul Dog finish talking in a bored-looking way to one of the Poor Souls and lazily indicate which way the client should go. The Poor Soul floated around the back of the desk and into what Quince recognised with a sudden burst of complete non-surprise as a toilet bowl.

There was a thin, ersatz flushing sound and the Poor Soul promptly vanished into nothingness.

"Hahaha," said Soul Dog.

"Awesome!" exclaimed Jeans, "That was, like, well funny, Soul Dog!"

"Yeah man!" added Roll-Up, "Classic!"

Slowly, the laughter died away. Quince was not laughing in a very prominent way.

"What," he said.

"Is," he said.

"The meaning," he said.

"Of this?"

"Um," said Jeans, looking at Roll-Up.

"Um," added Roll-Up, looking at Soul Dog.

"Um, yes," said Soul Dog, looking suddenly a little sheepish.

"You think this is funny, don't you?"

Silence.

"You think this is clever?"

Silence.

"You think you can just waltz in here and mess up a system that has been perfected over what is technically forever?"

Silence.

"You think…" began Quince, who was almost starting to enjoy himself by now.

"…your mum," muttered Soul Dog.

There was a horrified pause.

Then Jeans and Roll-Up collapsed into balls of helpless laughter.

"You think…" Quince tried to rally, but was drowned out by the catcalls of the two cackling Souls.

"Oh, you burned him, man!" shouted Roll-Up.

"Your mum thinks!" exclaimed Soul Dog, somewhat encouraged.

The other two collapsed once more at this masterly display of wit.

Feeling disturbed and suddenly out of his depth, Quince decided to change his tack.

"And look, what's with all this Lifey rubbish anyway?" he tried desperately, indicating the posters and the desk and Soul Dog's almost unbearably annoying hat, "I mean, if you lot are hawking Oblivion, why have all these cheap bits of Life stuff knocking around?"

The three Souls stopped laughing for just long enough to exchange a disbelieving look, before bursting once more into a derisive cacophony.

"Er, duh!" shouted Roll-Up.

"He's so dense, man!" Jeans chimed in.

"Yeah, it's *ironic*, dude," Soul Dog rolled his eyes.

"But…" tried Quince, who felt things slipping away.

"Move with the times, granddad!"

"But..." he said again.

"Life is so last paradigm,"

"Yeah, man, nothing is the new everything."

"But..." he tried, one last time.

"Your mum's butt," said Soul Dog.

And that was that.

Some non-time later, after the laughter had died down (or at least after he had gotten far enough away that he could no longer hear it) Quince realised he was not alone. A Poor Soul floated nearby, apparently trying to be unobtrusive and slightly comforting at the same time.

"There, there," it said to him, vaguely.

Quince stared at it sharply.

"What is it now?" he demanded, "Oh, have we decided I *do* have a use after all? Oblivion not your cup of tea now, is it?"

"No, I told you earlier, I wanted existence, please."

"Oh, yes, right," moaned Quince, suddenly remembering the Poor Soul he had met earlier, his last customer, "Well, I'm afraid existence is closed. Until further notice," he added grumpily.

Non-time passed.

Jamie Brindle

"What's your name?" Quince asked at length, mainly because there was little else to do.

"I don't know," replied the Soul.

"Very well. I shall name you..." Quince paused, "Bob."

"That's a shame," said Bob at length.

"No it's not, Bob's a very nice name!" exclaimed Quince, rather scandalised.

"I mean, it's a shame about existence. I was quite looking forward to it. Bob's a good name."

"Oh," said Quince, mollified, "Is it? Doesn't seem that many of you people are missing it much."

And just at that moment, there was a blinding flash of light, out of which stepped a short man in a faintly shabby grey two-piece suite.

"I'm afraid, Mr Quince, that you are rather wrong about that," said the man, "People are, in fact, missing it a great deal."

"Ah," said Quince, looking suddenly nervous, "I was afraid this might happen."

"Well," said the man, "Aren't you going to introduce me to your friend?"

Quince sighed.

"Yes, I suppose. This is Bob," He turned to the Poor Soul.

"Bob," he said, "This is God."

"What do you mean, 'revoke my charter'?" Quince exploded, "That's divine bloody law, that is! I mean, just who the hell do you think you are?"

"I'm God," said God, simply.

"*A* God, yes, of course, no question," Quince was trying desperately to keep his temper, "But don't get carried away with yourself, now!"

"There is only one God," said God, "We just have lots of little bits, that's all."

"Yes, and some of those bits are *very little*, I see," muttered Quince, "But, look, it's not my fault, OK? I mean, *they* were the ones who started the new business; *I* haven't done anything, have I?"

"Exactly," said God, "*You* haven't done anything. Some rivals move in, the whole of Existence going to rot and ruin, and what exactly have you done? Nothing, that's what!"

"Well," conceded Quince, "To be honest, I thought the whole thing would blow over in a couple of eons,"

"That's hardly the point," God pushed his horn-rimmed glasses back up his face; Quince noted without surprise that one of the arms was broken and held together with sticky tape, "The point is, down in Existence, not a child, *not one child* has been born since this nonsense started. You know why? I'll tell you why! No souls to fill the bodies! And that's just what's happening to Existence! Imagine the disturbances this is causing on The Other Side, and on Level Two!"

God rolled his eyes and made a little sniffing noise.

"When all's said and done, the whole thing's a ghastly mess. And that's why," concluded God, "I have been sent back here, back to the Beginning. To give you a little prod, as it were. Get the Souls flowing into Existence again, or your charter is officially revoked,"

"But," began Quince.

"No buts," said God sternly, "You're living on borrowed time, sunshine! Just you watch it, right?"

There was an implosion of light, and God was gone.

Quince was rolling his eyes, when God reappeared.

"Nice to meet you, Bob," said God affably, and vanished again.

Quince gave Bob a dirty look.

"Bugger," he said.

"This is so humiliating," muttered Quince, as they topped the rise and began drifting gently down towards the endless line of queuing Souls.

"Are you sure you don't want me to do the first bit?" asked Bob, kindly.

Quince scowled.

"No, no," he said gloomily, "It's *my* charter we're trying to protect. I should be leading this damn thing, I suppose."

They wandered a little way down-queue from the Establishment. Quince pointedly ignored the jeers and rude signs being made by Soul Dog and his cronies.

"So," said Bob after a while, "Should we start?"

"Yes, yes, I suppose so," snapped Quince.

He took a deep breath.

"What Do We Want?" he shouted.

"Existence!" Bob echoed.

"When Do We Want It?" Quince yelled.

"Technically Forever!" answered Bob.

The Poor Souls filed silently past. A few of them had the grace to look slightly abashed. Most of them just seemed indifferent.

After a while, Quince noticed that Soul Dog was coming over to them. He turned his back on the student Soul.

"What Don't We Want?" he thundered.

"Oblivion!" answered Bob.

"Why Don't We Want It?"

"A Fundamental Opposition To The Extinguishing Of Sentience As Opposed to A Constant Evolution Of Consciousness Towards A State Of Total Awareness!"

"That's very good," said Soul Dog, without apparent sarcasm, "Really catchy. Did you write it yourself?"

"Humph," said Quince, "Why are you so keen to know? Do you want to steal that, too?"

"My dear Quince, we are not enemies, just business rivals," Soul Dog grinned.

"Um, no actually, I think we are enemies," said Quince, with mock-thoughtfulness, "I can tell by the simple expedient of looking deep within myself, and recognising the vast and roiling sea of hate I feel for you. It's a dead give away, I'd say."

"My dear Quince..." began Soul Dog again, but Quince cut him off.

"I'm not your dear anything!" he snarled, "And while we're at it, what's with all these words of more than four letters you're using? When I saw you with your friends it seemed that your entire communicative repertoire consisted of asserting certain relationships between yourself and my mother. Not that I've got one, but still...And now that your two idiotic friends are nowhere to be seen, it seems you're suddenly capable of articulate discourse once more."

Quince glared at him malevolently.

"Well, the others, you see," Soul Dog looked embarrassed, "They don't understand...It's important to talk to them in language they are reassured by..."

"You mean you're pretending to be cool so they'll like you," said Quince flatly, "Typical bloody student."

"Well, anyway," said Soul Dog, visibly trying to pull himself together, "I didn't come here to argue. I just came here to let you know, the offer's still there if you need it."

"What?"

"The word from the Other Side is, you're in trouble," Soul Dog allowed himself to exude a smug little glow, "It seems Them Upstairs are unhappy with the way you've been running this show. Thought you might appreciate the offer. Why not take up with us? It's obvious your pathetic little protest isn't having much effect. As endearing as the placards are, of course."

Quince couldn't quite stop himself from stealing a guilty glance down at the board he was wearing. It read:

OBLIVION - NOTHING TO WRITE HOME ABOUT!

Soul Dog grinned.

"Yes, well," he said, "If you change your mind, you know where to find us. As I said before, we could use someone with your experience."

"Over my dead body!" yelled Quince.

"If your charter is revoked," rejoined Soul Dog, "It seems that is a distinct possibility. Farewell for now," he drifted away, before adding over his shoulder, "Or should I say: laters, dude!"

Poor Souls drifted past, but Quince did not have the energy to chant.

Jamie Brindle

"What do we do now?" enquired Bob, at length.

Quince sighed.

"Plan B, I suppose. Tell me Bob," he asked the small Soul, "Have you ever thought you might like dressing up?"

"But I don't want life anymore," protested Bob, "I quite like it here, I've decided. Can't I just stick around and sort of help you a bit?"

Quince rolled his eyes with exasperation.

"Look for the hundredth time, it's not a proper life OK?" Quince proffered the small life up for inspection, "It's just a little thing I knocked up, right? It won't take a moment, you'll hardly be gone at all. And it *will* be helping me, don't you see? This is Plan B! This is how we get the business up and running again!"

Bob looked uncertain, but he inched a little closer to the little life.

"Yes, that's it, that's it! Come on now, it won't hurt,"

Before Bob could change his mind, Quince suddenly thrust the life forward. The two connected, there was a brief flash of light, and Bob vanished...

...but only for a moment, and then he was back...

...only he looked rather different. He was still recognisably Bob – at least, when you knew that Bob was in there somewhere, and you actually *looked* for him – but he also looked like a rather podgy fellow in a black top hat, with wobbling jowls and a bulldog expression.

"What the devil was that?" Exclaimed Bob, "What the bloody hell am I wearing? And why on earth am I talking like this?"

Quince smiled. His plan seemed to have worked.

"Hey, you! Yes, you sir!" Quince pointed insistently at the random Poor Soul that had made the unfortunate mistake of catching his eye. The Soul was pulled inexorably towards Quince, where he stood behind his shabby makeshift stall.

"Ah, good of you to come to me!" Quince grinned, "Quite the right choice. Now, sir, I have a question for you: what on earth are you doing in that silly queue over there, when we have such *unbeatable* offers here?"

"Well," began the Soul, but Quince didn't give him time to answer.

"For instance," Quince continued, "Did you know that *right now*, and for a *limited time only* you can get not one, not two, but *three* lives for the usual price?"

"Really?" asked the Poor Soul, a glimmer of interest beginning to show through.

"Yes!" exclaimed Quince, "Imagine that – three lives! There are people down there who have frittered away their first life just trying to find a way of getting *one* more, and you could get *two extra* for free!"

Jamie Brindle

Another couple of Poor Souls had strayed away from the big queue, curious to see what the commotion was.

Quince swelled his chest and began to feel that things were not hopeless after all. It could work, it could really work...

"Well, I don't know..." one of them began.

"Well, of course you don't know," Quince jumped in quickly; this was what he had been waiting for, "You've never had a life, have you?"

The assembled Poor Souls shook their heads sadly.

"You *don't* know," he went on, "But I've some people here who would like to talk with you, some *very satisfied customers*, they'd like to tell you how absolutely wonderful my service is!"

Under the stall, he gave Bob a little kick.

There was a burst of light, and all at once the fat man of the black hat and bulldog face was standing next to Quince.

"Hello, my friends!" exclaimed the man, "I understand you are interested in taking a life? May I be the first to commend that choice!"

"And...who are you?" asked one of the braver Souls.

"A fine question," sang the man, "A great leader! I came when my nation called, and was honoured for it! And if you chose life, maybe you could do the same!"

"And tell me," said a new voice, "Was the whole affair sunlight and joy then?"

Quince looked up sharply.

"Bugger off, Soul Dog!" he said quickly, but it was too late; a cloud had already passed across the bulldog face.

"Oh it's not Soul Dog that bothers this one, Quince," said Soul Dog, "This one's got another dog that haunts his steps; and I'm not black"

"It is true, I must admit," the man stumbled over his words, "I was not always what you might call *happy*, exactly..."

He took a step backwards, head hung low, and he barely resisted as Quince swung him round and forced him into another of his pre-made little lives.

There was a flash.

The podgy fellow was gone; in his place stood a tall, elegant man with dark skin, a thick fuzz of black, tightly packed hair, a brightly coloured bandana round his head, and a guitar slung over his shoulders.

"Listen to me, baby," the man crooned in his rich, honeyed voice, "Life is sweet; take of that tree, and eat all you can,"

"Ah, yes," said Soul Dog, "And if you eat too much, well, that's what the vomiting reflex is for, isn't it?"

The man's guitar seemed to droop somehow, and all the fire fell from him.

Quince narrowed his eyes still further, and gave the man a shove.

There was another flash of light.

Now a woman stood there, with sultry lips and platinum blonde hair, and a skirt that danced and swirled in a wind that blew from an unseen grate.

"Take a life, boys," she smiled sweetly at them, and blew them a kiss, "Be born today, I'll sing you all your happy birthdays,"

"Ah, but nobody perfect, right?" Soul Dog sighed, "And all lives have barbs, my dear, do they not? Sometimes, lives end on those barbs."

"Enough!" shouted Quince. There was another flash. Bob looked about, confused.

"What...Um, what was that?"

"My point exactly," said Soul Dog smoothly, "Now come on children, you've had your fun," he began ushering the Poor Souls back towards the queue, "You see then, Quince? If that's the best Existence has to offer, then surely my Oblivion is better?"

Quince began to speak, but at that moment there was another flash of light.

Quince looked suddenly very sick.

"Well, Mr. Quince?" asked God.

"I'm..."stuttered Quince, "That is to say, I'm in the process of..."

"You mean you still haven't done anything, don't you?" asked God, not unkindly.

"Well, let's not be harsh on him," said Soul Dog, looking rather smug, "I mean, he *has* been trying. It's just that the simple and unavoidable fact is that his days are past. Change must be our watchword; nothing lasts forever, that's what we say."

God peered at Soul Dog over the top of his horn-rimmed glasses.

"We?" he enquired.

"Yes, me and my colleagues," Soul Dog went on, "We run the Establishment which has usurped Quince's little business."

"Ah, yes, I see," said God, warmly, "I must say, we have been following you people with some interest. You see, now that it seems Mr. Quince here has been unable to fulfil the terms of his charter, Us Upstairs have been looking at the alternatives."

"But..." Quince began in a thin, broken voice.

"Not now!" said God, quite firmly, and Quince drooped like a wilting flower, "Anyway, Mr., err, Dog, like I say, we have been looking at the alternatives, and well, it seems that we might be able to come to some sort of arrangement."

"How interesting!" said Soul Dog, smiling shark-like, "And how exactly do you see that working? We specialise in Oblivion, after all."

"Yes, yes, we are aware of that," God stroked his chin thoughtfully, "Well, the thing is, you see, that the Universe has been going on for quite some time now, getting bigger and brighter and expanding and throwing out billions upon billions of Souls...anyway, you know the picture, I won't bore you with the details."

"Of course," prompted Soul Dog, "Do go on?"

"Well, as things have worked out, your little Establishment has ended up bringing Us Upstairs round to questioning a few things. And it seems that we may have reached the Point of Reversal."

"The Point of Reversal?" echoed Soul Dog, intrigued.

Jamie Brindle

"Oh yes, the Point of Reversal," went on God, "It has been a theoretical possibility since the Dawn, of course, but no one ever really took it seriously. Until you boys came along, that is. You see, the very fact that you have been so wildly successful in promoting your Other Option could be taken as an indication that the Point of Reversal is due."

"And...what exactly does that entail?" Soul Dog was looking rather eager now, hungry almost.

"Oh, basically what it says on the tin, hahah," God gave a dry little laugh, "When the Universe reaches it's point of maximum expansion, there is a moment of absolute stillness, and then the whole thing starts running backwards. Lives stop being lived, children stop being born, the dead begin to, well, un-die, and that means..."

"That means," interrupted Soul Dog, "That means that all the souls who have ever existed, all the lives that have ever been lived, they all need to be...unmade."

"Bingo!" exclaimed God, "Ahahah"

Soul Dog swallowed.

"My God," he said softly, "We're going to be enormous!"

"Yes, I am," said God happily, "And yes, you are."

"This is brilliant!" said Soul Dog, "I knew, I always *knew* my idea was terrific!"

"Oh yes, so it would seem," grinned God, "Quite inspired, I must say,"

"Yes, I've always been very inspired," agreed Soul Dog, "A generally inspired Soul, that's me,"

"So all that remains, if you are amenable," said God, "Is for you and your colleagues to come and sign the necessary paperwork, and we can draw up the new charter. Which would make you *official*, of course."

"Yes, of course, of course," Soul Dog grinned, "But, well, do we really have to leave to sign the blasted forms? I mean, you can see how busy we are!"

He indicated the endless queue of Souls.

"Ah, I see your dilemma, yes," God frowned for a moment, but then his expression cleared, "But wait! The answer seems simple to me – why not just take on an extra pair of hands? After all, it hardly seems fair that someone like you, an ideas man as it were, needs to bother himself getting his hands dirty. Surely there's someone here who could work for you, and relieve you of some of the day to day tedium of your wonderful work?"

Their eyes met, and they turned silently to look at the forlorn Quince.

Soul Dog smiled.

"Well, he doesn't much look the part," observed Soul dog.

"That can be easily remedied," said God, and clicked his fingers.

There was a puff of smoke. Quince was abruptly wearing a garishly coloured tracksuit. On his head was a horrible little plastic-coated cap, with the logo of The Establishment printed on it in big bold letters. He was wearing a badge that said,

Jamie Brindle

Hello! My name is

Quince

Please can I take your order?

"Oh yes, that looks much better!" Soul Dog enthused.

Quince shot him a look that managed to encompass both bottomless bile and utter defeat.

"Come on now, Quince," said Soul Dog firmly, "Time to go to work,"

Quince followed God and Soul Dog as they led him to the Establishment. Roll-up and Jeans were working frantically behind the desk, sending Soul after Soul to the little porcelain toilet bowl floating in the middle of nowhere.

"Easy there boys," said Soul Dog, clapping his hands, "Why work so hard? Look, we've got a new employee!"

Roll-up and Jeans looked at the sad figure of Quince for a moment, and then collapsed into helpless fits of laughter.

"That's right," exclaimed Soul Dog, "We did it! We won! It's easy street for us now. Come on Quince! Get behind the desk and get stuck into your new career!"

Quince sighed. Slowly, he walked over to the desk and sat down with infinite misery on one of the chairs.

"Oh, and when you address me, remember to call me, 'boss'," Soul Dog added, gleefully.

Quince did not even have the energy to look disgusted.

"The controls are fairly basic, I'm sure you'll pick them up pretty quickly," said Soul Dog, "Go on, try pressing that button there,"

Quince reached out a tentative hand and pressed a little green button on the desk. The toilet flushed. For some reason, Soul Dog and his Colleagues seemed to find this immensely amusing.

"Ah, that's it, I knew you were a quick study, Quince," laughed Soul Dog, "Good work! Now," he went on, turning to God," you mentioned some paperwork that needed signing?"

"Yes, yes!" said God, "My counterparts Upstairs handle all the paperwork. I shall arrange transport for you...ah, directly!"

As he finished speaking there was a small sighing noise. They all looked around, to see an elevator descending slowly from the endless sky. It stopped in front of them, and its doors slid open with a nice little "ping" noise.

"Please, gentlemen," said God, indicating the elevator.

Grinning widely, Roll-up, Jeans, and Soul Dog trotted over to the elevator and stepped inside.

God shook each of their hands in turn.

"Wonderful doing business with you gentlemen," said God, "Send my regards to my people Upstairs, won't you?"

"Of course, of course!" said Soul Dog, a little peremptorily, "Now, how do we make this blasted thing work?"

"Oh, I think *I* can handle that for you, 'boss'," enunciated Quince.

Soul Dog just had time to glance out of the doors and shoot Quince a look of mixed confusion and fear.

"N..." he began, but at that moment Quince leaned forward and pressed the little green button.

The doors of the elevator slammed shut.

There was a thin, ersatz flushing sound.

The doors opened.

The elevator was empty.

Quince let out a long sigh and allowed himself a smile.

"He was right, you know," he said, cheerily, "The controls *are* fairly basic. And not too difficult to re-wire, I see. You can come out now, Bob."

There was a flash of light, and God disappeared.

"Oh my," said Bob, "That was an interesting one!"

"Yes indeed," agreed Quince, who was busy getting rid of the desk and the chairs and the posters and all the other trappings of the Establishment, "It was like I said – having a 'plan B' is all very well and good, but sometimes the thing it's most useful for is making them think you don't have a 'Plan C'."

"It almost makes me wonder if I wouldn't like to try a whole life," went on Bob.

"Well, that's what I'm here for," said Quince merrily, as he put his old office back together. He checked his desk, and was happy beyond words to find all the lives piled up there as usual, just waiting for Poor Souls to come and live them.

"Although," began Bob uncertainly.

Quince stopped moving things around and looked at him.

"Yes?" he asked.

"Well, the thing is, you see," Bob stammered nervously, "I wondered, um...well I thought, you're going to be awfully busy now, after all that business, and I sort of wondered if maybe..."

"Yes?" Quince asked again.

"If maybe you needed an assistant?" Bob looked at him hopefully.

Quince smiled broadly.

"Bob, my friend," he said, "Welcome on board."

The End

Echoes

When my father's father returned from the war, he walked straight past his young wife and the small baby she held in her arms, and would not talk to her for a month. He was convinced that she had been unfaithful while he was sleeping in the mud and watching blood bloom amid the dirty, sandy sea of French beaches. He was convinced the baby was not his own. Though he eventually resumed communications with his wife, the new baby – my father – was never shown any affection, or even interest, and it was not until four years later, when my uncle was born, that my grandfather expressed any emotion for either of his children,

Before that there were no fits of rage, no uncontrolled storms, just a steady, freezing stillness that settled around the new family like a second skin. When my uncle came into this world and started screaming, the moist air from his hot little lungs brought the first touch of thaw to a four-year winter.

Forty years passed, and I was born.

At my uncle's funeral, I hunch my shoulders against the tepid English rain and hold my grandmother's hand. I don't know what to say to a woman who has just had to bury her son. She looks small and birdlike, delicate in her black clothes and simple ornaments, but she is tough: tough as old boot leather, tougher than me. I am not crying. I don't feel like crying, though I feel that maybe I *should* feel like crying. I was never close to my uncle.

The casket is in the earth now. The guests are taking it in turns to come forward and heap spades-full of sodden dirt into the ground.

Splat. Splat. Splat.

My father steps forward and grasps the spade. His hair is silver now, almost white, and he wears glasses he never needed when I was growing up. But he is still strong, still energetic. He goes for long walks in the afternoon and sometimes climbs up and down the stairs fifty times when the weather outside is grim.

There are no tears in his eyes. He looks more angry than sad.

Splat.

The ceremony is finished, and we go back to the men's club that has been hired out for the reception. The smoking ban has just come into force. This room is meant to be wreathed in tendrils of cloying tobacco fumes: it is used to the obscurity this usually offers, both to vision and to olfaction. There is no smoke now to hide the faded yellow plaster of the walls, to hang over the odour of musty carpets and six generations of beer-soaked Saturday nights. The light seems too bright; the buffet spread out on a tablecloth on a threadbare pool table looks like the final specimens in a tired police investigation.

I play pool and darts with my brother and the cousins we haven't seen for ten years. We smile and offer awkward consolations, promise to not let it be so long before we meet again, try to find one another, try to bridge the gap.

My father is floating round the room, recognising his dead brother's friends, trying to reconcile his recollections of faces in the illusionary Cinefilm sunshine of memory with the stark, lined, fleshy things before him. They are like inverted ghosts of who they used to be, as if the past was the dream, vivid and Technicolor, imagined up from these figments of pallid reality. He collects stories and sometimes laughs but never cries.

I stand by my mother, beautiful and beautifully solid in her serious dark jacket and smell of clean competence. This is the mother I remember from my childhood: the solicitor who held the family's dealings with the outside world and always new what time the trains would arrive. She has been in retirement for fifteen years, resting while it was safe for the other mothers to come out for a while; but she is needed now, and so she has returned. We put our arms round one another's shoulders and watch my brother beat everyone at pool. This is natural: he is a snooker player – just like his grandfather – and the table looks small and unimportant to him, like a toy or a broken puzzle. It grows dark outside and at last it is time to go.

I sit in the front of the car on the way home, next to my father. My mother and my brother are in the back, flanking my grandmother, who has decided to come and stay with us for a few days, until the first sharpness of grief has been blunted a little.

"I can't believe he's gone," my grandmother says once or twice, to no one in particular, to all of us, to the world.

My father tells the story of the time, when they were children, that he thought he had killed his brother. He had thrown a dart into the air – up, up, up catching the sparkling sun which always shines so brightly in the past – and down again into my uncle's skull. There is a moment's stillness, an indrawn breath, screams, blood.

"But he always had a thick skull," my father finishes, with a half-smile, sad, and the first hint of moisture near the corners of his eyes.

"There was no telling him to do anything," my grandmother agrees.

"Just like you," says my brother, and we all smile, because he could just as easily have been talking to my father, or my grandmother, or to himself.

I fall asleep early that night, but wake in the middle stillness between one day and the next, when all the world is in darkness and all you can hear is the motorway fifteen miles away carrying the shallow, midnight pulse of sleeping London out into the fleshy green tissues of the country. I dress in silence and float towards the kitchen, sip a glass of water and peer out into the shadowed garden.

Someone whispers my name, and it is half a heartbeat before I remember my grandmother is staying with us. She is in the room next door.

I move into her bedroom and stand at the foot of the bed.

"Is that you?" she asks, suddenly uncertain, and for a moment so am I, as if in the darkness I could be anyone, my uncle, my father, my brother, the echo of my grandmother's voice.

The sensation passes, and I sit down on the mattress and take my grandmother's hand.

"I couldn't sleep," I explain, and she squeezes my hand.

A faint wind blows outside, *swish-swish-swish* through the branches of the apple trees, and I can smell the rich Autumn scent of apples ripening to rot on the muddy ground. The cats will be out tonight, the last two descendants of a feline dynasty that extended from the vague, sun-dappled time before my birth up to the present day and will end soon, with the current generation, germ lines severed by a trip to the vet when the prospect of eternal cats began to trouble my ageing parents. All my childhood was filled with cats, so many that I cannot now enumerate them, they dance and fade in my memory. Sometimes there were only two or three. Sometimes there were so many that you could never be sure how many there were – though they numbered in the dozens – or if you would find one in the shower or under the table, playing with your toes, or creeping onto your face at night with little explosions of catty breath to warm your ears. An endless parade of cats, marching from their hidden, secret nests in the garden and out onto the main road, where countless cats died.

Now there are only two, and I wonder if they are sad, if they know they are the final expression of a theme that has played again and again through the apple-littered grass, and which in this ultimate manifestation are indistinguishable from the unnumbered generations that have gone before.

"They were so different, as children," my grandmother says, and for a moment I am confused, because surely she should have said, "They were so different, *as kittens*," and then I realise that she is talking about my father and his brother.

"How were they different?" I ask, though I know the answer already, have been told it a thousand times.

"Your father was so quiet, so...so easy, no trouble, always good as gold,"

I smile in the darkness, and if it hadn't been this night, if we hadn't just buried my uncle I would have said, "So when did he change so much?" like I always do, because the thought of my father being quiet and no trouble is always hilarious.

Instead I squeeze her hand again and ask, "And what was his brother like?"

"Oh, your uncle was always a terror!" she chuckles, a dry, scratchy sound, like sandpaper on smooth wood, "He'd never do what he was told. I thought I was going to die when he got his motorcycle! He scared me half to death."

When they had turned eighteen, both my father and my uncle had been allowed one expensive gift from a generous relation. My uncle had chosen a motorcycle, while my father had gone for a complete set of the *Encyclopaedia Britannica*. I don't know where my uncle's bike ended up, but my father's books are still in the living room, faded leather behind murky glass cabinets, dreaming golden dreams of a time before the Internet.

"But then, your father was in hospital," she goes on, her voice clouding, drawing back in, "Perhaps that's why he was so easy. He was in the hospital for months, sometimes,"

My father had asthma and double pneumonia as a child, and was an inpatient on the edge of death for a long time, until a newly invented drug called "penicillin" saved his life. My uncle never had pneumonia, but he smoked more than my father.

I wonder what the house was like during those long months when my father was in hospital, watching the victorious Lancasters, the glorious Spitfires and Hurricanes chase white clouds across the blue sky, through the narrow, grubby window at the foot of his bed. I wonder if my grandfather thought much of the son he did not accept as his own, wonder if he laughed with my uncle while my father was away, whether he took him on his shoulders to the men's club and taught him how to hold a snooker cue, while smoke wreathed his face and stained the walls yellow.

We sit in silence for a long time, so long that I begin to wonder if my grandmother has fallen asleep, and how best I can leave the room without waking her. But then she stirs and speaks again.

"Your grandfather was awful to your father," she says at last, as if our thoughts have been running side-by-side, a pair of parallel trains in the darkness, "But your father was wonderful at the end,"

The year before I was born, my dying grandfather had come to stay with my father and his wife in their new house. My father had held the old man (who was younger then than my father is now) and fed him and dressed him and cleaned the shit from him as his fading body had slowly shut down. I don't know what forgiveness had passed between them, in this final chapter before I was even conceived. One book was closed and another was opened; or maybe someone just flicked to a different page.

We talk some more, about inconsequential things, then I say goodnight and head back to my room. A faint noise catches my attention. Dawn is greying the fields outside my window when I open the curtains to discover the source of the tapping, and see two feline eyes staring in at me. I open the window, but the noise scares my visitor away. A gentle drizzle is falling, a background to the noise of the waking world.

I fall asleep and dream of hospitals.

I wake the next morning and follow the smell of coffee to the kitchen, where I find my mother listening to the radio and eating poached eggs. Noises from elsewhere in the house suggest that I have been the last to awake. I smile at my mother and give her a hug. She has a few more lines around her eyes, but her hair is as black as when I was a child, and when she smiles it is as if the years telescope back into themselves, as if time is an almost palpable illusion linked to the muscles of the cheek and temple.

Click-click-click, from the large games room, and I know my brother is awake, playing a miniature game of snooker on the old pool table we are lucky enough to own. I follow the noise, and find my father bent over the table, lining up a shot, while my brother stands in the half-open doorway, tapping cigarette ash into an October wind that is trying to seep in and sweep the room to Autumn. My mother has enforced a strict no-smoking policy throughout the house, but at times of stress or celebration, this ban is relaxed to allow smoking on thresholds and out of open windows.

My brother looks thin and taut. The light catches him in a certain way, and for a moment the feeling of uncertainty that touched me last night sweeps me up again, and I am not sure if I am me looking at my brother, or my father looking at my uncle, or my grandfather looking at his son, or what page of the book is being read from at all, at all.

Then I see the red round my father's eyes and his kind smile, and I know that he is my father, and who my brother is, and I know who I am again.

I kiss my father on the cheek and put my arms around him.

My brother extinguishes his half-finished cigarette on the wall outside, closes the door and comes back to us.

The End

The Bound Book

Advance Directive

My name is John Price AD, and I have to decide if someone lives or dies. That's my only job, that's why I'm here, that's my goddamned raison d'etre, pardon my French.

If this particular person hadn't popped a clot out of his heart and got it lodged in his brain, subsequently wound up on the stroke ward of the local District General with no movement in his right side and not much in the way of consciousness either, I wouldn't be here. Literally.

I can't go and touch this poor bastard, can't hold his hand or shake his shoulder myself, can't try and reach him physically. But I've got a whole shed load of different camera views from my little room, and I can see it's pretty much a hopeless case. He hasn't really woken up, not since he's been brought in. Sometimes his eyes flicker open and stare blankly at the camera on the left – not to the right, I'm not even certain he's really aware of what *right* means anymore – sometimes he moans or cries. But there isn't much light behind those eyes, that's for sure. They're feeding him by a tube that goes down his nose into his belly, because the muscles in his throat don't work properly anymore, and if he ate anything, half of it would probably wind up in his lungs.

All in all, the guy's in a pretty shitty state, as I say.

But it's a tough call to make, tough as hell.

That's what I'm here for. That's what he wanted, what *I* wanted I should say.

That's why I was constructed, from his brain twenty years back, when it was young and optimistic, and didn't have a big gaping chunk of necrotic white matter rotting away on one side like a worm in an apple.

It's tough waking up one day and realising you're not real.

It's even tougher seeing what you've become, and then having to decide whether to pull the plug.

Karen's not really supposed to talk to me – that's one of the rules – but I can watch her, and she knows I'm here. She was the one who persuaded John Price – the real John Price, that is; not John Price AD, i.e., me – she was the one who persuaded him to have the advance directive made.

I can remember it clear as glass, of course I can, just as clear as I can remember every other significant event of my simulated life. It was around the time her father was dying. He didn't have a stroke, he had dementia, but hell, same difference at the end, really. We went to see him most days for what seemed like forever, but it was probably only a couple of months. Most of the time he didn't even recognise her, didn't even register her presence. Sometimes he cried out and talked to people who weren't there. Most of the time he just blinked, looking confused and kind of hurt, then got on with the business of pissing and shitting himself.

Karen wanted them to pull the plug, but they couldn't, of course. They could withdraw some treatment, they told us, but it was another thing entirely to stop feeding him, stop giving him fluids.

It wasn't their decision to make, they told us, and it wasn't Karen's, either.

"Bullshit," said Karen, "I was his little girl, for Christ's sake, he raised me and changed me, I was closer to him than anyone, you think I don't know he would have hated this?"

But it wasn't in their hands or ours, and it took several long weeks for him to die. When he started coughing up green phlegm and struggling to breath, Karen was so happy.

Right about that time, the whole advance directive thing was getting fashionable, at least if you could afford it, and we weren't doing so bad.

So we got scanned, we both did.

And that's how come I'm here, watching myself living a vegetable existence, live through the thousand and one electronic windows of my digital cage.

I wouldn't want to go on, if that was me, I keep catching myself thinking. And then I realise, *shit, that* is *me*!

This whole damn situation is just too fucking weird.

Karen brings the children, and that's weird as hell, too.

Tommy was only four when John Price was scanned, and Grace was just a faint swelling around my (his) wife's belly. Now my kids are young adults; I missed their whole lives. I can kind of recognise Tommy, the tilt of his chin or something. And I can see myself in Grace, too; our eyes are the same.

I try and imagine what it must have been like, watching them blossom and grow. I have access to a whole library of videos and photographs, birthdays and holidays and so on, but it's not the same, of course it isn't. I review these archives, try to feel some connection to these children, but it's like grasping mist; and I feel like I'm spying on them, too. Are they really mine? Sort of. Yes. No. I'm not sure.

Tommy holds John's left hand – they keep the right one under the blankets because it's horribly swollen and stiff, don't ask me why – and gets excited when the hand twitches back. It doesn't mean shit. I can *see* it doesn't mean shit. This poor bastard might as well be dog food, might as well be a fucking jellyfish for all the awareness of his surroundings he has. But all Tommy can see is that his Dad squeezed his hand, and suddenly there's a treacherous glimmer of hope in his face.

Karen strokes her/our son's head, and looks straight at me through one of my cameras. Her eyes are hard. What is that there? Defiance? Resentment? *Hate?*

I take my time to come to my decision – shit, I'm not gonna rush into killing myself, am I? – but there's only one way I can jump, really.

I wouldn't want this, and I'm based on him.

Ergo, John Price would want the plug pulled. Case closed.

I log into the system, and enter my choice.

Except, it turns out the case isn't closed at all.

Karen knew which decision I'd come to – she had lived with me for close on twenty years; even after the divorce there was some contact, or at least, that's what the records give me to understand. The point is, she knows how I think (or maybe that should be *thought*?), and she had an objection order in place just waiting for me.

Which means, this is not going to be a clear cut case of me saying my future self would want to pop his clogs, and then vanishing myself in a puff off evaporating electrons.

If I want me dead, I'm going to have to fight for it.

I can't get over how real this all feels. Just like real life. My lungs move, fill with air. I can hear sounds, taste and smell and touch things. And the so-called 'real' world can see me, too. We're just separated by an endless sequence of thin glass sheets, that's all. I'm trapped in a cage made up of all the computer screens in the world.

Karen is in front of me, standing behind what looks like a thin glass window. Up till now we haven't been able to talk to one another. Now that the case is going to the courts, the rules are different.

I don't have to justify my decision to kill John Price. Of course I don't. That's not the moot point. As his walking, talking advance directive, I have complete powers of advocacy over his life. I had them from the moment it became doubtful if he would ever regain a significant degree of consciousness, at which point my files were dusted off and my simulated self was switched on.

No, Karen couldn't make a case around whether I'm making the right decision or not. That wouldn't wash at all.

What she can do – *has* done – is to attack my right to existence *at all*.

"People change," she tells the jury, "When you leave this hearing today, you won't be the same people you were when you arrived this morning. Every experience changes you. Every thing you learn, every thing you see and hear, every event in your life, however marginal, all build up in you, changing you. We are, all of us, in a constant state of *becoming*."

It's obvious where she's going with this. Other people have tried similar things in similar cases. Sometimes it has worked, sometimes it hasn't.

"That simulation of my ex-husband that you can see standing just behind the TV screen is *not* my ex-husband," she goes on, "It's a simulation of the man John was *twenty years ago*. The fact that as of this moment no law exists that automatically nullifies advance directives after a given amount of time has elapsed – and one could argue that even *five years* would be too long a time – the fact that no such law exists is just one example of how poorly thought out and bound in law the whole science of simulated advance directives has been, and continues to be."

Karen was always good at talking. She's better than she was when I knew her, much better. I wonder what the woman I love has been doing with herself these past twenty years to get so much more confident, so much smoother.

That's something else that complicates the situation, by the by.

I love her.

I can't help it. John loved her when he was scanned, so I love her now. The fact that she's put on some weight and has more grey in her hair than brown doesn't change a thing.

I love her. I love her, and she hates me.

It's my turn to talk now.

I address the jury, not Karen. Matter of fact, I can't even look at Karen. I can't stand to see the contempt in her eyes.

"Karen Price is trying to convince you not only that I'm not really real, but also that I am an inaccurate simulation of the man I was based on," I begin. I am struggling to keep my voice steady, struggling not to notice the way Karen is looking at me.

"I can't attempt to argue the first charge – though I can tell you it feels pretty Goddamn real – but I'll give the second my best shot. Yes, everyone changes as they go through life, of course they do," I carry on, "But that doesn't mean that we become different people, not literally. Elements within us change, but the core of us does not. I'm here because John Price didn't want to go on living if he ended up as a vegetable. That wasn't something John changed his mind about. If he had done, he could have logged into his account and deleted me with the click of a button. The fact that he didn't means that, despite twenty years of life experience existing between him and me, *we are still essentially the same person*."

Karen says some more after that, then I go again, but the thrusts of our arguments have already been laid out, and it's basically a matter of recapitulation, of trying to win the jury over with different ways of saying the same thing.

After a while, a bell goes off, and we have a recess.

Karen asks to see me privately during the break, and I hesitate for the whole of about a second before clicking the button and accepting the request. Big mistake.

She asks me directly to drop my decision, to resign my position as advocate, to let John Price live.

"Karen, can't you see that he doesn't *want* to live?" I ask her, "I wouldn't want to, and I *am* him, for Christ's sake!"

"You arrogant prick," says Karen, "Don't talk as if you're really him. You're not him. You're nothing but lines of code churning away in a motherboard somewhere. When this farce is over someone will press a button, and that's that, you'll be gone, no ashes, no funeral, because *you're not real.* And I'll tell you something else, I hope to hell the person who gets to press that button is me."

"Shit Karen, when did you get so fucking bitter?" I say, because something is breaking in me, "You were never like this before. Never nasty like that, never so fucking nasty."

I realise my voice is breaking, too, and the tears running down my face are obscuring the video screens. They even simulated the damn *tears* right.

When I look up again, something has changed in Karen's face. I think maybe she's crying, too.

"Jesus, John, don't you think this is hard for me, too?" she whispers, "To see you again, to see how you were, before things went wrong..."

She trails off, then starts up again.

"You look exactly like he did," she says, "You look like him, sound like him. The way you talk...It's like meeting a ghost. It's just like meeting a ghost."

Then she puts one hand out and touches the screen. I reach out to her, but all I can feel is cold glass.

"The kids...Tommy...he can't bear to see his father go like this." Karen is not quite looking at me as she speaks, "There was a lot of bad stuff between them, at the end. After the divorce, things got pretty messy. If he was to go now...look, maybe John won't wake up. Maybe he won't. But if he just hangs on a little longer, maybe that'll give Tommy the chance to...I don't know. To say some things, even if there's no one listening. To make peace with himself, or...or something."

I can feel my resolve caving in. I love her. How can I say no to her? She wants me to hold off on my decision on account of her/my son.

I run a hand through my hair.

"Look," I say, "Look, OK, I'll hold off. For the moment. If Tommy needs some time, then OK, we'll give him some time."

Also, it'll give me some time, too. I suddenly realise that maybe I'll have a chance, not only to get to know the woman Karen has become, but also to get to know my kids. To get to know Tommy.

"Thanks, John," she says. She half-smiles at me. I nod, and kill the connection on the computer screen.

Her face flashes and is gone, replaced by a familiar view of John's hospital room. I watch his chest rise and fall, slow, laboured. A doctor comes and stabs his good arm with a little needle so they can put another bag of fluid up, to keep him from dehydrating and dying while I refuse to make the decision that he would want, but that the woman I love does not. His hand jerks a few times, and the doctor calls a healthcare assistant to pin the arm down while he gets the needle in position.

His eyelids flutter briefly, then still.

Jamie Brindle

I'm not scared of dying. I know that sooner or later I'm going to be pulling the plug on John, and when I do that I'll basically be pulling the plug on myself, too. Us advance directives do not enjoy the right to live beyond the souls who made us.

There's a catch, though, to stop A.D.'s from choosing to keep their "real" counterparts alive as long as possible, just so that *they* can go on "living" (in this weird, digital sense) themselves as long as possible.

You get a couple of weeks to make you choice, then either way, that's that buddy, time's up for you.

Say I decided to say, OK, John Price would want to go on living, don't pull the plug. I'd make my choice, throw my two cents in the ring, then I'd be switched off, just the same as if I'd decided to pull the plug. Goodbye John Price AD. The only difference is, if I decided to keep him alive, I could be re-awoken again if there were any change in his condition. If he deteriorated, for example, say he had a second stroke or something, then I'd be brought back to reassess, to see if I felt the situation had changed significantly.

But am I afraid of dying? Why the hell should I be? I don't even really exist, as people are so fond of pointing out. Truth is, I *am* a ghost. The real person is either dead or dying, depending on your point of view. Fuck it, if I think about these things too long, my head starts to hurt. And that pain feels pretty Goddamn real, thank you very much.

There are other things I'd rather spend these precious remaining ghost-moments on than a killer of a headache. Like watching my son, for example.

126

He comes to see John most days, more often than Karen does.

He mostly just sits by the bedside and doesn't say much. Sometimes he holds John's good hand. One or twice he tried reading to him, but I think he felt self conscious about it, and he didn't do it for long. It's a book I used to love when I was about Tommy's age, about a kid with some kind of developmental problem who has an operation to make him smart. It's funny, I used to run myself round in circles thinking about who the *real* kid was – was he the idiot or the genius, or who? Which version would he be when he died and went to heaven?

Now that the court case has been resolved, I'm not supposed to talk to Karen or the others again. But it's not an actual *law* – as Karen said, the laws surrounding the use of simulated advance directives *is* ridiculously lax – and I can't help myself in the end.

"What are you thinking about, Tommy?" I say through a speaker one day, when I can't stand his endless sad silence a moment longer.

He doesn't jump, doesn't even start. It's as if he knew I was there all along – of course he knew I was there, where the hell else would I be? – and was just waiting for me to say something.

He doesn't reply for a long time, and I begin to worry that maybe he won't say anything, that he has decided to follow the rules and not interact with me at all.

"I'm thinking...how did things change to end up like this?" he says eventually, "When I was a little kid, we were so close. I used to have nightmares about what it would be like when you...when he died. I used to get really worked up about it. Then I used to run and hug...him...I used to hold him so tight. And now, this. Sitting in a hospital room, and not being able to say anything...I'm not even sure the last time I hugged him. We... fought a lot, since the divorce. Since before the divorce, really. So I guess I'm thinking about how point A gets to point B, when there isn't even really a single moment I can point to and say, that's it, that's when things changed."

The silence stretches on.

"Was I a good father?" I ask eventually. I have to.

"Yes. You were." I can see the tears starting to form in the corners of his eyes. "You were a great father. I loved you so much. Whatever happened afterwards, you were a great father."

He gets up suddenly, leans forwards and kisses John on the forehead. Then he turns around without another word and walks away.

Karen comes to the hospital the next day, but she doesn't come to see John, she comes to see me.

"Tommy says he spoke to you," she tells me, "I think it did him good. I don't think he's going to visit again."

There is a long pause. I know what that means. I know why she's here.

I wonder if I should ask the question I am dying to ask. Is it fair? But then, I'm going to be gone soon, probably in a few hours at the most. Why the hell shouldn't I ask her?

"Could it have been different, Karen?" I say, "I guess...thing's looked so rosy. Did it have to end up this way?"

"You shouldn't forget, we had good times too. A lot of them." She wipes the corner of her eye. "Things run down in the end, one way or another. Things end."

"I wouldn't have fucking let things get this bad!" the words jump out, before I can call them back. I should stop, it isn't fair to talk to her like this, but I can't rein myself in.

"How could he have hurt you all like this, ruined everything, fucked everything up so royally? I want to kill him. I want to kill him, Karen. I want to switch us both off."

She smiles so sadly. She kisses my screen. Now there's a smear of lipstick on the glass, and the world is blurred.

"It's time to go, John," she says, "But please, don't do it in hate. Do it, but not in hate. There were good times, I promise you. You did good things."

She leans over the body in the bed, and kisses him on the forehead, too.

Then she stands up, shakily, and walks out of the room.

She is right. If she can forgive him, why shouldn't I?

I type the code in, and this time there is no counter-instruction waiting there from Karen.

John is about to die.

I wonder if computer simulations go to heaven.

After all, does God really give half a damn about the difference between a neurone and a diode?

Maybe there's every version of every possible person in heaven. All the people we could have been if we went left instead of right, or had one less beer before driving home, if we had seen things through rather than giving up on them.

Something flickers, and all the screens go dark.

The End

Jamie Brindle

His Hungry Little Children

And then they were kissing, and Harry was too drunk to tell her that he didn't really want her, that he didn't even really like her, that the fact they had ended up alone together in the upstairs bedroom was an accident and not his design.

Her moist lips sucked at his skin, smothered him, covered him in fierce kisses. His hand slid down, and felt the small muscles of her buttocks tense underneath the thin, fatless layer of skin that covered them.

For one moment he stopped, pulled back, hesitated. From downstairs, the last sounds of the dying party crept into the room. The light from a street lamp outside the window caught the angle of her chin, glanced off the sallow skin of her cheek, lit up the hunger in her eyes. She looked... afraid, almost. Did she sense his hesitation?

Harry teetered on the edge, torn between stopping things before they went any further, and plunging on regardless.

Outside, a midnight train rattled by on its way towards the city. A wave of small-town loneliness swept him up, chilled him, and plunged him forward into the ugly warmth of her open arms.

Fuck it, he thought, and tried to push the image of her long, plain face out of his mind.

"We call her Picasso," he told his brother the next day, by the time they had reached their third pint, "Because when you look at her straight on, it's as if you're still looking at her profile."

Harry laughed at his own joke, but his brother only smiled, a little sadly.

"And are you going to call her?" Luke asked.

"Yeah, like fuck I am!" Harry snorted, "I'm going to have enough trouble living this one down, even if no one ever hears from her again! Call her? Of course I'm not going to bloody call her!"

"How is it you know this girl, anyway?"

Harry shrugged his broad shoulders.

"She's just...about, you know? We see her down here every now and then. She's usually on her own. Occasionally some poor sod gets drunk enough to take her home. God knows what she was doing at the party."

"And last night, that poor sod was you, was it?" Luke asked, smirking.

Harry rubbed one hand across the stubble on his face and yawned.

"Yeah, I suppose so," Harry grinned, and tipped his brother a wink, "Must have had a few more than I intended."

"She certainly gave you a few kisses to remember her by," laughed Luke, pointing at the many love-bites that covered Harry's face like dark butterflies.

Harry frowned at that. When he had first caught site of his face in the mirror earlier he had got quite a shock. The bruises were ugly, wide swellings underneath small scraps of broken skin. Picasso had been a passionate kisser, that much was certain...

Luke took a long pull on his drink and set it down, empty, next to his brother's.

"Well, that's me done for the night," he said, "If I'm not back by ten, Emily won't let me back in at all."

Harry started to smile, but the grin froze on his face.

"Shit, that's her!" he whispered, ducking back behind his brother.

"What, your Picasso?" exclaimed Luke, twisting around and craning his neck to see, "Christ, I see what you mean!"

Luke turned to Harry, who had pulled himself back into the little booth they were sitting in, trying to make himself as inconspicuous as possible.

"What's she doing?" hissed Harry, "Is she looking for me?"

"Ah...I don't think so," said Luke, peering between the dense fog of Saturday-night bodies that littered the pub, "She's just...I think she's just ordering a drink."

Slowly, Harry shimmied himself back up in his seat and looked over at the thin girl by the bar.

As his eyes locked on her body, a wave of nausea washed over him. He thought about how recently he had lain next to that sour, yellow skin, thought of the stiff, jagged hardness of her bones as they moved beneath her hot flesh. She was wearing a shapeless grey T-shirt now; but he knew that beneath it lay her protruding ribs and the buds of underdeveloped breasts, could see them in his mind's eye. The scent of her was in his nose again, damp hair and the cloying trace of some rotting femininity that had clung to him through three showers earlier that day, and which had only finally been smothered by a long bath.

"Come on," he said, "Lets go."

They had almost reached the door when, prompted by a treacherous urge he could not resist, Harry's head swung back round towards the bar.

She was sitting on her own, bony arms leaning into the sticky, drink-stained wood, propping up her long face. Her straw-like, dirty brown hair hung loose around her neck and dripped into the glass of black liquid she had ordered.

She was looking at him.

Their eyes locked, for just one moment, then she turned away.

Harry blinked.

"She blanked me," he said, bemused, as Luke pulled him outside.

His brother laughed and slapped Harry on the shoulder.

"Look's like you're not as irresistible as you thought!" Luke said, already walking away towards the street where his wife and his dinner waited, "I suppose she wasn't that desperate after all! See you later, mate."

"I suppose not," agreed Harry, trying to find the smile he knew he should be wearing, "Have a good one mate, I'll call you in the week."

Luke waved over his shoulder, but Harry was already making his own way home, troubled by something he could not name.

He awoke in the stillness of the night, soaked in sweat, and rushed to the bathroom in time to bring up the vomit into the toilet basin. Cramps wracked his body and brought him to his knees. At last, the contractions faltered and passed. He laid his hands on either side of the porcelain and pushed himself upright, wiping sour liquid from his mouth. The toilet bowl was filled with his sickness. It was stained with bile and vivid streaks of blood. Appalled, Harry wiped his mouth clean, pulled the flush and slammed the lid down, covering the churning water as it washed away his fluids.

He pulled himself unsteadily to his feet and staggered back to his bedroom, where he fell back into a dark, dreamless sleep.

The next morning, his skin was covered in blisters. They were everywhere: on his face, his arms, nestled in the sweaty black hair in his groin, even distorting the inside of his mouth. He could feel a small one under his lower eyelid. There was another under his foreskin. There were hundreds of them.

He felt sick, but ravenously hungry too. He wanted to go out and spend all his money on food, but he was terrified of anyone he knew seeing him like this, so instead he ransacked the random contents of his depleted cupboards. He ate half a tub of margarine, raw, and three eggs that he was sure smelt sour and unhealthy. He scraped the last few ounces out of an old plastic packet of self-raising flour, mixed it with sunflower oil and salad cream and stuffed it into his mouth. It all tasted delicious, but it did not seem to fill the hole in his belly.

By the time he had eaten everything in his apartment, the sun was well on its way down the sky again, and Harry began to wonder about making an appointment to see the doctor. He looked in the mirror, hoping to find the blisters had gone down, but when he stripped naked and examined himself, he found that if anything they had grown larger.

He grasped the biggest one he could see, nestling on the end of his chin and the size of a two-pence piece, between his thumb and forefinger, and gave it an experimental squeeze. He winced. Just touching it even slightly sent a bolt of pain through his face.

He braced himself and brought his fingers together as hard as he could.

Harry screamed as agony exploded in his face.

The blister crunched open. Blood and pus splattered onto the surface of the mirror. Something solid bounced off the glass and down onto the carpet, where it glistened wetly.

Harry leaned down, cradling his burning chin, and peered at the bloody thing that had come out of his face.

A small, high pitched, rattling noise came from the glistening mass. He could just make out a tiny mucus-covered face and four delicate foetal limbs.

The thing jerked twice and was still.

Harry wrapped it up in toilet paper and flushed it away, horrified.

He looked at himself in the mirror. Underneath the thin skin of the blisters, he fancied he could see small movements.

His breath came in ragged gasps.

He rushed to the kitchen and scrabbled about for the sharpest knife he could find.

This time he chose one of the blisters on his arm. He stared at it. Already it looked bigger than it had done, bigger than the one on his chin.

Tears were stinging his eyes. His face was throbbing with pain. How many more were there? There must be *hundreds*.

He forced himself to lay his arm flat on the work surface. Carefully, he brought the knife down until it was just touching the surface of the blister. Even that light brushing was uncomfortable. He breathed hard.

Something underneath the blister slapped against the surface of his skin.

Harry stabbed the knife down into his arm, and screamed as fire swept through his muscles.

He felt the knife slide through the blister and down into the healthy flesh of his arm beneath. Watery blood seeped up through the incision, drained away down the side of his wrist. Something jerked on the end of the knife. He looked closer. A small body was impaled through the chest, transfixed by the knife to the flesh of his arm. Tiny legs jerked back and forth in spasms, and a thin keening noise hissed out from an ugly little mouth lined with minuscule black teeth. Appalled, Harry withdrew the knife and held it up to his eyes, unbelieving.

The small creature writhed and spat on the end of the blade. It had thin, tiny arms; and when it looked at him, he recognised her eyes.

He dropped the knife and the vile thing that was stuck there.

A fresh pain had begun to build in his head, behind his eyes. There was a pain in his chest too, a growing pressure that he had not noticed until now.

He staggered towards the window.

Something shifted in his groin. He felt something tear, and a wetness dripped down his leg. He looked down. The blister in the fleshy fold between his thigh and pubic hair had burst of its own accord. Something was pulling its way out of his tissues. He could feel its lithe little body scratching against the bones of his pelvis.

He reached down and snatched at the thing, but it darted and slithered away before he could catch hold. This one was fully formed and mature. He caught a flash of its horrible sharp teeth before they bit into his thigh and tore away a little chunk of his flesh.

There was more pain in his back now, more wetness. More of the blisters were bursting.

There was a sound from outside, a voice he recognised. He lurched towards the window, and felt something ripple within his head. Suddenly, the right half of his body went numb. He tried to scream, but his face felt strange and slack, and he couldn't move his mouth properly.

He slammed against the window, managed somehow to leaver it open, and looked out into the gathering twilight.

A strange cooing noise floated up from the street below.

All over his body, he felt the blisters flutter and rend, as the creatures within buzzed and quickened.

He looked down.

She looked up at him, thin and ugly and strange.

He shuffled out onto the window ledge. Something was wrong with his eyes now, and he could feel his lungs being eaten away from the inside. There was no room in them anymore to draw breath.

Harry leant forward and allowed the meat that had once been his body to topple out into the night.

In the twilight strangeness of the street, the thin, ugly father sang a feeding song to all his hungry little children.

The End

Red In Tooth And Claw

'So careful of the type?' but no;

From scarped cliffs and quarried stone

She cries 'A thousand types are gone:

I care for nothing; all shall go.'

...

No more? A monster then, a dream,

A discord. Dragons of the prime,

Who tare each other in their slime,

Were mellow music match'd with him.

-Alfred Lord Tennyson,

"In Memoriam"

The sun was sparkling on the river and the wind was blowing through the pines and life was not fair.

Catherine watched sullenly as her two young wards splashed in the water, jumping and squealing and chasing each other from rock to rock as

they made their way down the winding course of the shallow stream.
Jayne was her sister – well, she was *half* her sister – and although she was
only four years younger than Catherine they had never been close;
Catherine thought of her always as a burden, never a blessing.

A bird cried out in the trees above, and Catherine squinted up into the
sun, looking over the steep path down which they had descended to reach
the river earlier that day; then she looked at her watch and sighed. It was
still only just past noon, and a good four hours before her parents were
supposed to meet them at the bottom of the small mountain.

She snorted and forced herself to scramble down the mud and shingle
after the younger children.

"Don't go so fast!" Catherine commanded, "I don't mind if you break
your neck, but mum and dad will, and I'm the one who'll have to explain to
them why their favourite little brat isn't prancing about under everyone's
feet!"

George hesitated at her voice, and looked over his shoulder, worried.
But Jayne did not take any notice – when had she ever? – and grabbing the
boy's hand, she pulled him along after her. Soon they were out of sight,
but she could hear their wretched giggles echoing up the valley walls,
mingling with the soft riffle of water on water on stone.

Why had they ever dragged her along to this ghastly place? It simply
wasn't fair. Perhaps she would not have minded if she had been allowed to
bring a friend, like Jayne had. She could have brought Grace or Lilly or
Sarah...or even Robert, now that might have been *really* interesting...Not
that any of her friends liked walking or trekking or bloody *climbing* any

more than she did, but they could have stayed in the little cottage her parents had rented while the others went out, and maybe worked out some way of obtaining some of her mothers "secret" supply of gin.

But no. Of course not.

Jayne could bring her little boy-friend, but there were only five seats in the car, after all, and no room to think about what might make Catherine happy. When they had announced this holiday to her, this stupid week away trip to the Lake District, Catherine's first feeling had been elation, and her first hope had been that she would be allowed to remain at home while the whole of her wearisome family departed: the house to herself for a whole week! But her father was having none of it, and as his face remained stern and resolute as she passed through pleading, cajoling, anger, and eventually tears without noticeable dent in his resolve, Catherine had gradually realised that her fate was irrevocably sealed.

A week of boredom and walks and sores on her ankles.

Not to mention babysitting her stupid little sister and her stupid little sisters friend, of course. Mum and dad had organised the whole expedition, but it would have been foolish to assume they would want anything to do with their children. Oh no. They would much rather shift the burden of care to Catherine's shoulders and stay in the silly little cottage without MTV or even a CD player and do...what? Catherine shuddered at the thought of her parents, naked and flabby, lounging on the starchy white sheets, cigarettes and gin on the bedside table, and quickly cut it off before it could finish forming.

She sighed again and rolled her pretty eyes theatrically to herself. She shouldered her rucksack and set off after the others.

As the river wound its way deeper into the valley, the grassy walls that bounded them in on either side grew taller and more sheer. Rocks and little caverns began to poke and gape from the sides where before only grass and daisies had been, and the flow of water was strengthened by a thousand minute tributaries that slunk from underground pools or reservoirs, unseen in the hillside, but dripping and echoing their way along like snakes.

Jayne and George had abandoned their game of jumping from stone to stone in the water, after an unfortunately slippery chunk of rock had given way beneath Jayne's feet and unbalanced her. She had grabbed wildly for George, and they had both gone careening into the swim. Jayne had squealed like a plump little pig, and for a moment Catherine had smiled to herself, thinking the stupid girl had sprained her ankle and might stop playing and laughing so annoyingly. But it didn't take long before she was up on her feet again, dashing with George back and forth on the bank and drying out quickly, fighting and jousting with branches dry as bone from the midday sun.

At last, the path levelled out somewhat, and the river emptied itself into a small, still tarn. The walls of the valley receded to either side for a little way, before bunching themselves up again and following the river as it continued out the other side of the miniature lake and off down the mountainside. The ground on either flank of the tarn sloped upwards a little, and to the left a series of small cairns were arranged in ragged alignment. Catherine followed their line lazily with her eyes. Strange. It looked as if they got bigger and bigger as they got further from the lake. The nearest one could hardly have been piled higher than her waist; but the next one was almost as tall as her, and the one after that looked as if it must have been taller than her father. Frowning slightly, she let her eyes wander on along their course. The last one was piled as high as her house, and leant very snugly right against the rocky side of the valley wall. Near the top, the mountainous wall gaped open in a wide crack, black and empty.

Catherine's head snapped back at a squeal from George.

"Hey Jayne," he yelped, "It's really warm! Feel how warm the water is! Let's go for a swim!"

"Oh no you don't," Catherine shouted back, "You've already got yourself wet once today, I don't want mum complaining to me that I let you catch a cold!"

Jayne pouted her lips for a moment, and Catherine thought she would put up a fight. But George looked embarrassed, and Catherine saw Jayne was wavering.

"I'm going to sit down and have a rest," Catherine went on, pushing her advantage, "You can follow the river down a little way, but don't go too far."

They hesitated for a moment.

"Or you can sit here with me and be nice and quiet," she offered warningly.

That was enough for them. Not even waiting to say goodbye, the two younger children sped off towards where the river continued on its way on the far side of the tarn.

Soon they were out of sight, though Catherine could hear their shrill voices echoing up the valley walls and through the trees.

When she was sure they had gone, Catherine settled herself carefully on a large, dry rock by the tarn, facing away from the line of cairns and towards the still water. She unhooked her rucksack and began to rummage around inside, and pulled out a series of treasured items: first, her new mobile telephone; then her sweet little make-up kit (bought for an extravagant sum from a high-class shop in Oxford street, under heavy – but ultimately futile – protestations from her mother); last, and most humble-looking, a battered carton of cheap cigarettes she had persuaded Robert to steal for her the night before she left.

She played with the buttons on her mobile phone, and soon it was blaring out a tinny, plastic tune at a volume which seemed utterly improbable for something of so diminutive a size. Catherine smiled slightly, and placed the phone carefully on the rock next to her leg. A flock of little blue birds took offence at the noise, and darted away from a bush they were hiding in to search for more serine environs. Catherine paid them no mind, and after lighting a cigarette, she snapped open her make-up case and began to inspect her face in the mirrored lid.

It was as she had feared. The heat and bright sun of the day had caused her make up – so carefully applied this morning before they set off – to run and flake. She looked a mess, a horror! This would simply not do. She balanced the make up case on the rock next to her mobile phone, and began trying to restore at least some degree of beauty to her ruined face.

After a few minutes, some of the worst damage had been undone, and Catherine was beginning to feel as if the situation was not altogether without hope, when she started to get the strangest sensation that she was being watched. At first it was so subtle that she hardly noticed it, just the faintest prickling between her shoulder blades. She shifted uncomfortably, and glanced around; but there was nothing amiss that she could see. Apart from her phone, the world was very silent; no birds were singing, and even the constant whisper of the river into the tarn seemed muted. Frowning, Catherine turned back to her mirror. She tried to concentrate on her face.

Her lipstick was fixed now; so was her eye shadow. One eyebrow was looking rather messy. She selected a fine brush and began to dab at it.

Swish, swish, swish...

A rock shifted on the scarped cliff behind her, and she whipped her head about to face the noise. A pebble was bouncing down the mossy hillside. She turned back to the mirror.

A young man dressed all in white was reflected in the glass, standing looking at her, just behind her right shoulder.

Catherine cried out and sprung to her feet, knocking the makeup case, her mobile phone, and her cigarettes all into the cold water. The tinny music issuing from her little pink phone was abruptly silenced.

She whirled around, her heart hammering at a thousand miles an hour.

There was no one there.

She glanced about nervously. There was not a soul in sight.

The only sound was the final, muted thuds made by the little pebble as it finished its desultory descent from the cliff and rolled to a halt by her feet. She hesitated for a moment, then reached down and picked it up. It was only small, and fitted nicely into the palm of her hand. It was elongated, and tapered to a ragged break at one end, while the other finished in a pair of smooth domed caps. If felt light in her hand.

Catherine stared suspiciously back at the large cairn, and the gaping black crack etched in the cliff face above. The wind stirred around her, and for a moment she almost fancied she could hear, very faint and far, a voice, or voices.

It sounded as if they were singing.

Suddenly, she remembered her prized possessions, all wet and floundering now in the water at her back. Forgetting everything, even the stone she held in her hand, she whipped around and went down on her knees, lunging desperately for the phone. The water was only shallow, and she scooped it out easily, but when she looked at it she groaned. It was dripping wet, of course; water was even pouring out of the little speaker and microphone holes at either end. The screen had gone blank, but had also taken on an ominous oily, rainbow sheen. Without much hope, she jabbed half-heartedly at the buttons. Nothing happened. Feeling like crying, she tossed the phone lightly onto the grass, and bent back to fish out her cigarettes. They were equally ruined, sodden and bloated like a line of little white corpses with yellow foam heads. She crumpled them up in her hand and threw them away, furious.

Last of all came the makeup box. It was sitting on the bottom of the tarn looking quite serine and undisturbed, and for a moment Catherine held onto a breathless hope that it was undamaged. But when she reached down to pull it up, she felt a sudden pain in her hand, and she pulled her arm back, gasping. A great red shadow was blooming on her wrist and running down her arm.

A moment later, she realised that the mirror must have shattered and the broken glass been sticking up towards her; she had lacerated her arm on it. Dark red blood welled up through the sharp cut. It pooled on her arm and dripped down into the still water of the tarn. Catherine followed the first drop of blood with her eyes as it flowed off her arm and down towards the water. It hit the surface and bloomed instantly into a crimson rose; and at that moment, time seemed to catch, somehow. She saw the blood rippling out through the tarn; and at the same time she saw herself, but not as she usually saw herself, confident and worldly and tortured half to death by the vagaries of an uncaring world and the depredations of foolish parents and a selfish sister. Instead she saw a young, pale girl with uneven makeup and a weak chin.

And behind her, again, was the man.

Her breath caught in her throat. The moment seemed to stretch away

into forever. He was young and tall and beautiful, and he wore a white

hood – though through the reflection of her blood it seemed crimson – deep

over the pale, perfect skin of his face. A shock of ebony hair stood out in

sharp contrast to his white skin, and fell in a gleaming ponytail down

beside the delicate line of his jaw. The flesh of his chest was bare

underneath the rich folds of a cassock as pure white as his hood, rich with

muscle and smooth as sunset. One arm was lost in the voluminous folds of

the cloak, but the other was reaching round, around *her*, brushing past her

slim waist, with a strong hand reaching out towards hers. It was holding

the strange pebble, too. Her vision blurred, and for a moment she had the

sickening sensation that the two arms were one, and she could not tell

where her hand ended and his began.

Her sight cleared, and she could perceive his hand clearly again. It was

stretching for her, reaching closer, closer, closer. Her heart was beating

wildly. Her lips trembled.

He was so beautiful.

She leaned towards him.

Someone shouted, and the frozen moment shattered.

Once again, she spun around. Once again, she was alone.

She stood tensed, too frightened to move, too terrified to make a sound.

Her breath came in hard, ragged gasps. A thin moan, half longing, half

loss escaped her lips. For a moment, all she knew was a burning

disappointment that the man had gone; and tied to that, a wrathful loathing for the shrill shriek that had interrupted them moments before they could touch.

Then the shout came again, and all at once recognition flooded through her.

It was her sister's voice.

She was screaming.

Catherine tore along the narrow path, brushing aside long trails of brambles that blocked her way and not caring as they tore at her hair and scratched her skin. The path weaved backwards and forwards next to the river, and she could never see more than a few yards ahead of her. Suddenly, the screaming stopped. Catherine halted for a moment, uncertain. Then she plunged forward once more, scrambling along the path with renewed vigour.

The way twisted back on itself once more, and all at once it opened out again into a larger clearing, similar to the space with the tarn, except there was no pool here. Instead, the stream seemed to shrink in on itself, becoming all at once much more drained and feeble than it had been but a few moments before. But the sides of the valley opened up very wide, with walls that were sharp and steep, and looked almost as if they had been hewn straight with tremendous force by some terrible spade or shovel. The sides of the cliff were made of layers upon layers of stone – flint and marble and slate; and here and there amongst them, deposits of some substance that looked very white and cold. The layers were ragged and uneven, and at irregular intervals shelves projected out some way from the otherwise flat cliff edge. It made Catherine feel like nothing so much as a tiny ant shuffling along the bottom of a sort of natural building site.

She caught her breath.

On a shelf, maybe fifteen feet up from the dusty ground, and only attainable by some perilous ascent from ledge to narrow ledge, sat Jayne and George, backs tight against the wall.

Below them, peering up from beneath his crimson hood, stood a bent old man, skin thin and yellowed under his red robe, ragged white whiskers unclean on his face.

He's just a monk, she thought, trying desperately to calm her hammering heart, *Like the ones who live in the mountains in Asia somewhere. He can't hurt you. He's probably taken a vow of silence or something. And he's only an old man! Why are you so afraid?*

But with his long red robes and sallow face, he looked like no other monk Catherine had ever seen.

"Hey!" she cried out, and the word was still dying on her lips when she saw the wolf. At least, that was the only thing she could think the creature might be. It was standing by the red-robed feet of the strange monk, baleful yellow eyes glaring up at her. It looked like a wolf, but it was gaunt, oh so gaunt. She thought she could count every rib that strained out against the tight flesh. It lowered its head and growled at her, and Catherine found herself hesitating.

It can't be a wolf, she told herself, *All the wolves in England are dead. It's just a dog, just a skinny, mongrel dog*.

The monk turned slowly to face her, and Catherine found herself wondering if perhaps the old man was deaf, because it seemed to her that he had not turned at her shout, but rather on sensing somehow the unease of the creature by his side.

He looked at her a moment with knowing eyes.

Fear sank in on itself and folded back to anger in Catherine's belly.

It was his fault Jayne had screamed. His fault the beautiful man in white had left her.

Suddenly she was striding towards the Monk again, arms swinging warlike by her side. She brushed her hand against her leg, and it stung where the mirror had cut her earlier, and that made her more angry still.

She couldn't leave her stupid sister alone for five minutes without her getting into some trouble! What if her mother were to find out that she had let some old, silly monk chase her up a cliff side? No doubt it would be she, Catherine, who caught the brunt of the parental wrath.

She glared at the monk as she approached.

"What do you think you're doing?" she demanded of him; but he just stared back at her, and there was a stillness in his eyes which checked her for half a step.

She looked down before she could stop herself; paused for a heartbeat; forced herself to look back up. Ignoring the monk, she stopped a few paces from him and directed her gaze at her sister.

"What are you doing up there?" she shouted, "Are you scared of this stupid dog?"

She tried to force scorn into her voice, but even to her ears her words sounded flat and powerless. Beside the monks side, the creature began to growl low in its throat. Catherine forced herself to keep her legs rooted to the spot.

"No," Jayne called back to her, sounding petulant, "The man's wolf scared the other man away. It was the other man we were scared of, we climbed up here so he couldn't get us,"

Catherine frowned. She could feel the Red Monks eyes boring into her, but she refused to meet his gaze. In fact, she was not sure she *could* meet his gaze, even if she wanted to. Better to forget about that, and focus on the children for now...

"What other man?" she shouted up, frowning.

"He was all in white," George volunteered, "And he said he wanted..."

He stammered to a stop, looking embarrassed.

"What did he want?" Catherine demanded.

"He said he wanted us to kiss each other," shrilled Jayne, "He looked nice, and he was smiling, but he didn't *sound* nice, so we climbed up here. He told us to come down and kiss each other, but we didn't want to,"

"Then Jayne threw a rock at him," George sounded impressed, "But he jumped out of the way,"

"But it made him angry," Jayne went on, "He said something horrible to us and...and I felt tight, right here," she pointed to her throat.

"Then we started to scream," said George, "And then this red man and his wolf came, and the white man got scared and ran off,"

"It's not a wolf," said Catherine, "All the wolves are dead,"

"How true," said the Red Monk, and the world seemed suddenly very quiet.

As she turned to face the monk, she thought she heard the creature growling; but then she started: the dog – or wolf, or whatever it had been – was gone. Where it had stood there were just bones, a small pile of alabaster bones. The noise was just the sighing of the wind in the trees.

"Who are you?" she demanded, but her voice sounded thin and weak in her ears.

The Red Monk said nothing for a very long time; and when he did speak, he did not answer her question.

"But this whole land belonged to the wolves once," he started abruptly, as if continuing some old conversation, "Hundreds of them, packs and packs and packs of them. They covered the whole of England, before England *was* England, when it was simply a land of hills and valleys and rivers and stars above the oak trees. They ruled here for a time, the wolves; and then men came, and all at once they had England, and before they knew what that meant they had a King and then they had a Parliament and an Empire and Income Tax. Now they have Burger Kings and Parliament TV. And the wolves died, and all that remains now are their bones, frozen in the earth and stone and fading memories of the world."

The wind picked up, and the sun sunk behind a cloud, and Catherine's hair fluttered and danced in the darkening substances of evening.

"Well, that's very interesting..." she began, but the monk twisted suddenly, quicker than she could have imagined. He whipped out his arms and grasped her hands in his.

"Careful, girl," he growled, a warning tone in his voice, "Be careful with your thoughts, be careful with your choices. The children have been lucky today: strong and brave...but mostly lucky. Others walk these hills but me."

He turned her hands over, and although he did not press hard and nor did her hurt her, she felt she could have resisted him as easily as she could stop the turning of the world.

He was looking at her hands, and she followed his gaze. In her left fist, clenched tight and forgotten, was the pale pebble she had picked up from beside the tarn. Her right was stained red from where she had cut it, but it had scabbed over and was no longer bleeding.

The red monk nodded to himself.

"Blood," he said, "Blood and bones. That's the choice, as it always is. Or...are they ever really to be chosen between?"

He let her hands fall. She fingered the pebble – only of course it wasn't a pebble, it was a *bone*, it seemed obvious now that he'd said it – and slipped the little white thing absently into one of her pockets.

The monk looked away slightly, over at the treetops with eyes that seemed to be peering elsewhere.

"But before the wolves came, there were others," he went on, as if he had never interrupted himself, loud and steady, "Other creatures, large and small and fast and slow. Some were weak. Some were terrible; but in the end they made way for the wolves, as the wolves made way for the men. Wolves and men and blood and bone.

"Who will the men make way for, I wonder?"

Catherine stared at him. Her lip trembled, and suddenly she did not want to be here, with this stupid, frightening old man and his strange words. She thought of the handsome man in white she had seen reflected in the mirror and in the tarn. She snapped her eyes back to the ledge.

"Jayne," she barked, "George. Come down now. It's getting late, and we have to get going or we won't be in time to meet mum and dad,"

George slithered from the ledge, and jumped nimbly down from rock to rock to stand beside her. He shuffled his feet and refused to meet her eye.

But Jayne lingered, and when she did deign to descend, she did so slowly.

Catherine could feel the Red Monks eyes on the back of her head.

"Come on, Jayne!" she hurried her sister along.

She wanted to leave before the monk said anything else.

But when the monk did speak, it was not her that he addressed.

"You did well to climb away from the man in white," the Red Monk said to Jayne, "And better not to listen to him when he called to you. Pray do better still, and be gone swiftly,"

Jayne hopped down and stood facing him, looking up into his withered face.

"He looked young, but his voice was old," she said.

"That he is, child," said the monk, "As old as sunlight. As old as these hills. Do not go back to him."

"Come on Jayne," Catherine's voice was brisk as she seized her sisters hand, and started to pull her away, "We're going now,"

Jayne let her sister pull her along, and George followed, but she kept her eyes on the man in red.

"You look old, too, very old," she said to him.

The Red Monk's mouth cracked in a faint smile.

"Me?" his chest moved in a silent chuckle, "I'm as new as spring. And as ancient."

Catherine tugged Jayne away, and the three of them moved off, following the river down the mountain. She was glad they were getting away from this strange place and the strange Red Monk. She was sure she could feel his eyes on them as they picked their way amongst the rocks towards where the clearing narrowed again to a path.

But when she realised she had left her rucksack back by the tarn and snapped her head over her shoulder, the Red Monk was nowhere to be seen.

"We shouldn't be going this way!" Jayne protested for the hundredth time, planting her feet and stamping one for added effect, "The White Man is this way, we should be going down!"

Catherine gave her sister's arm a savage pull, and dragged the smaller girl along in her wake. George followed sheepishly after, looking pale as chalk.

"Don't be such an idiot!" she chided, "There's no-one here! That old man in red was just trying to scare you! Anyway, I just need to get my bag, then we can go."

"But the *White Man* is at the lake!" insisted Jayne, as if that somehow explained everything.

"There is no one at the lake!" Catherine shouted back.

But wouldn't it be nice if he was *there?* Catherine thought to herself, *Maybe he is there, with his white clothes and white teeth and beautiful white skin...*

"Maybe we could wait here?" suggested the timid George.

Catherine shot him a look of contempt, and he actually stepped back a pace.

"No one is waiting anywhere," said Catherine firmly, "We'll just go to the lake, I'll grab my bag, then we can go…"

But just then they rounded the last corner to see the tarn spread out in front of them, and her voice trailed off.

There was the rock she had been sitting on, sure enough – she could even see a splash of bright red where her blood had stained the dusty stone – but of her rucksack, there was no sign.

Catherine halted, with Jayne and George a half-step behind her.

"Where's it gone?" said Catherine to herself, looking around blankly.

"It doesn't matter, we should just go!" said Jayne, at the same moment as George pointed towards one of the cliff edges and exclaimed, "There it is!"

Catherine spun to look at him, and followed his pointing finger with her eyes. Her eyes leapt from one barren cairn to the next, higher, higher, until there, finally, far up and catching a glint of the unseen sun, she saw her rucksack. It was balanced on the very furthest and tallest mound of rocks, on the very edge of the gaping black hole in the cliff face against which the cairn nestled.

The wind whistled through the rocks and the dying day felt cold.

What on earth was her bag doing up there? She had left it not twenty feet from where she now stood, sitting on the rock by the tarn, warm in the sunshine.

"Someone must have moved it," she said, almost believing it herself, "Probably some kids came past and thought they'd put it up there as a joke,"

"There hasn't been anyone else!" Jayne protested, and George nodded mutely by her side, "If there had been, we would have passed them on the way back here!"

"Don't be stupid," Catherine rolled her eyes, "They probably went back up into the hills. Or they heard us coming and hid in the bushes, don't tell me you haven't done something as stupid as that before. Now be a good girl, and run up there and fetch it for me."

"I'm not going up there!" said Jayne firmly, "And neither is George!"

Catherine stared at them a moment, undecided.

"Fine!" she said, "If you're too scared of heights, then I'll do it!"

And without another word she turned on her heel and strutted off towards the cairns.

After she had gone a few yards, Jayne called after her.

"Catherine! Don't!" her shrill voice sounded thin in the emptiness, "What if the White Man's there? Lets just *go*!"

Catherine ignored her sisters voice.

The way was steeper than it looked, and by the time she had passed the third cairn, Catherine was hot and breathing hard. She could feel sweat pooling under her arms and running down her thighs, and her shirt was sticking to her moist back.

But strangely, the closer she got to the cliff edge and the tallest cairn, the more energy she felt she had. Her heart hammered and heaved in her chest, but her muscles felt springy and strong and her body was tingly and light.

She came to the base of the final cairn, and peered up. She could just make out the edge of her rucksack, high above her, with one black clasp dancing in the wind. Her ears and face and throat felt strange. She arched her neck backwards and yawned, and for a moment coloured spots danced in eyes and her ears popped as if she were rushing into a tunnel on a train, the fastest train she had ever ridden on.

She stumbled, and for a moment she thought she was going to fall. She put one hand to the ground to steady herself, and took a deep breath, and another, and a third.

She looked over her shoulder, back the way she had come. Jayne and George were quite close really; but it was strange, because at the same time they seemed to be half the world away. She thought they were shouting something at her, but she couldn't hear what they were saying.

She heaved herself back on to her feet. Her breathing sounded very loud in her own ears. Gingerly, she reached out a hand and placed it on one of the rocks that formed the great cairn before her. She saw that her hand, her whole arm, was shaking.

She felt so strange – scared and sick and dizzy – but excited too, somehow. She touched the roof of her mouth with her tongue, and delighted in the rough stickiness of the texture. She bit down hard, and felt the tender flesh resist for a moment then burst like a sultry fruit. Warm blood filled her mouth. It tasted delicious.

She reached out her other hand, and slowly at first, then moving faster, then moving with almost frantic speed, she began to pull herself up the cairn.

When she reached the top, she slithered her sweaty body onto the rock face and leant against the cliff wall, panting. She stared up at the sky. The wind was very strong up here – it whipped her hair about her in a storm, and her sweat froze her face as it dried.

She thought being still would calm her frantic heart, but if anything it was beating harder now. She looked around blankly. Where was she? What had she come here for? Why did she feel so excited? It was as if all the birthdays of her childhood had come at once; and yet she could not remember why she should feel like this.

What was that object? It looked familiar. She should know what it was.

Oh yes. It was her rucksack. She pulled herself over to where it was laying, and clumsily unclasped the top. She reached inside.

What was she searching for? Her hand grasped something that felt familiar.

In starts and jerks, she pulled the object out of the rucksack. It was her makeup case.

She flicked the catch with a trembling thumb, and the top sprang open.

It took her a moment to recognise her own face in the mirror.

She looked so pretty. No, not pretty.

Sexy.

Her mouth was gaunt and her face was pale and sweaty and her lips were red with blood. But she looked *hot*. She smiled, and her sexy reflection smiled back.

But wait, that wasn't right. Hadn't she broken the mirror? She frowned, and leaned back slightly to ponder the matter. Her sweat-soaked shirt rubbed against the rough stone of the cliff face, and the mirror shifted in her lap.

And she saw him there behind her, in his tight white cassock as pale as winter.

She gasped and half turned. He was gone.

She turned back to the mirror. He was there.

Her whole body ached for him. She watched with baited breath as his reflection reached out for her. His hand touched her shoulder and gripped her tight, so tight it hurt, so tight she almost screamed with the pleasure of it.

She moved her own hand up to touch his; but where their flesh should have touched, there was nothing. She felt so frustrated she wanted to die.

"No, my sweet," his voice was honey and deep water, "Not yet. I am too weak to be yours."

"But," she stammered, "But I *want* you!"

Jamie Brindle

"Of course you do," she saw his teeth flash a hard smile in the mirror, "And you shall have what you want. But first we need strength. The strength of youth. We must have...the children."

For a moment, Catherine did not know what he meant. Then an image of Jayne's face seemed to explode in her mind.

She shook her head.

"They stayed down by the lake," she said, "They're afraid of you. They won't come up."

"Oh, yes they will, my sweetling," he said, "Call them up."

Catherine crawled forward on her belly until she was looking down at the little valley. She could see Jayne and George, they were standing by the lake looking up at her. They looked a hundred miles away and as clear as still water at the same time.

"Jayne!" she cried out, as loud as she could, "George! Come up here!"

She could not see the man in white anymore – she had laid the mirror carefully on the rocks – but she could hear his breathing in her ear, could feel his warm breath on her cheek.

"That's right," he was saying, "Call them. And lean forward. Do not be afraid; I will hold you."

Catherine edged forward. A rock gave way beneath her, and went tumbling down the cairn, bouncing away amongst the loose pebbles.

Jayne gave a cry and jumped to her feet. Catherine gasped and smiled. The world span around her, and she closed her eyes. When she opened

them, Jayne and George were standing straight below her at the foot of the cairn, necks arched back, staring up at her.

Jayne was shouting something, but all Catherine could hear was the wind (or was it her blood?) roaring in her ears. Jayne pointed at her and gestured and stamped her feet.

"I can't hear you!" Catherine shouted down, the words feeling thick and ungainly in her throat, "Come up here, then we can talk!"

She spread a hand and reached down towards the children, feeling somehow that if she could only stretch hard enough she could reach them no matter how far below her they stood, reach them and pluck them up and set them down beside her.

Another rock shifted under her, and she lurched down. For a moment she thought she was going to fall, and she cried out involuntarily. But she had only slipped a little way before she felt him, his strong hand pushing hard in the small of her back, pinning her immobile to the lip of the cairn.

Jayne cried out again.

"No, wait!" she screamed, "Stay there Catherine, stay there and we'll come and help you! Come on George!"

And without a backwards glance, Jayne began to scramble up the rock face.

George hesitated a moment, and then followed.

"Well done, my sweet," she felt his breath hot against her face, tasted his sour-sweet air in her mouth, "Soon we shall have them,"

Catherine writhed her hips against the stone, and smiled as she felt the bones of his hands pressing hard into the flesh of her back. She flicked her tongue, and watched as a bright spot of blood plummeted down through the air and landed on Jayne's upturned face. The younger girl did not seem to notice, so intent was she on her climbing.

She watched a few moments longer; but when Jayne was no more than ten feet below, and George only a few paces behind her, the Monk shifted his hand on her back and spoke again.

"Now, come back," he breathed, "Bring them back to the cave,"

She tried to scramble to her feet, but the strength seemed to have leeched from her limbs, and she half fell back to the rock face. Then his strong arm was looping under her body, pulling tight on her ribs and small breasts, drawing her upright and then back into the cave, the dark, dark cave against which the cairn leant.

A few paces inside the entrance, his hand abruptly loosened, and she half stumbled, half fell to the rocky floor. The air was very cold in here, and a strange wind seemed to blow incessantly backwards, as if air was being drawn in from the mouth of the cave and away into the darkness, as if the whole mountain itself was breathing. But Catherine did not feel cold in the cold air; her body seemed on fire, every sinew and fold of her flesh seemed to sing.

"I need you," she tried to say, but the words would not come.

Still, he must have heard her, for she felt his hand brushing the hair out of her eyes, and, "Soon," he was whispering to her, "Oh, so soon..."

"Catherine!"

It was Jayne, her head rising up suddenly, silhouetted against the sky through the entrance to the cave.

Her eyes were red raw; she had been crying.

She advanced unsteadily to the lip of the cavern. A moment later, George rose up behind her, and came to her side.

"What are you *doing*?" Jayne wailed, "Come *on* Catherine, we need to *go*!"

"Bring them closer," he whispered in Catherine's ear.

Catherine raised a shaking hand, and beckoned her sister.

Jayne shook her head.

"No!" she shouted, "Something bad's in here, something really bad! Come back with me."

For a moment, Catherine was at a loss.

"It must happen soon," his voice whipped like a hissing snake in her ears, "Soon, or not at all!"

Catherine sucked in a breath and staggered to her feet.

She could not let her sister spoil it all, not again.

At first, Jayne looked relieved; but when Catherine approached closer, she saw something was wrong, and her smile vanished.

"Give me your hand," Catherine commanded, but Jayne shook her head sullenly.

"Give it to me!" Catherine repeated.

Jayne thrust her hands behind her back, but it was not her hands that Catherine lunged for, it was her hair, her sister's long, yellow hair. She gripped it tight in her fist and yanked on it cruelly.

Jayne screamed and stumbled forward into the cave.

"Good," she heard his voice whispering next to her ear, "Good. And now...the boy."

Catherine looked up, and saw George was watching her, fear in his big round eyes.

She held out her free hand.

"To me, George!"

When George hesitated, Catherine gave Jayne's hair another vicious tug, and her sister cried out again.

"No, don't!" he said quickly, "I'll come, don't hurt her!"

And with that, he shuffled into the cave too, and held out his hand, and Catherine took it and pulled him close.

As soon as George was by her side, it felt to Catherine as if the whole mountain shuddered beneath her feet. She reached out a hand to steady herself, but *he* found it instead. Her hand seemed so delicate and small in his, so frail.

"He's here!" Jayne shouted, "It's him, the Man in White!"

She tried to pull away, but Catherine found she could hold her quite tight with nearly no effort at all. George just stood there, mouth open, eyes moist.

"Make her be silent," the Man in White commanded, and almost before she knew what she was doing, Catherine let go of her sisters hand and struck her very hard across the face.

Her sister crumpled to the ground, weeping.

Catherine could barely contain the pleasure that pulsed through her.

"Now," she whispered, "They are here, now, won't you...?" she felt suddenly coy, and could not finish her sentence.

But to her relief, she realised that nothing more needed to be said. The Man in White was reaching a strong arm around her waist, pulling her close, crushing her against his body.

His mouth loomed close to hers. His breath was on her lips, between her teeth, rolling on her tongue, sickly-sweet decay and sex.

It was beautiful.

He kissed her and the world stopped.

She felt the breath drawn out of her, felt her heart hammer out all the beats her life had to offer, as if all the years of her existence, the years that lay ahead of her, everything that she was and could be, all was haemorrhaging away into the dark of the cave.

Her skin felt tight.

She shuddered in ecstasy. It lasted an age and a moment and no time at all.

All at once, the joy was gone. Her skin sagged back and felt lose.

Her lungs felt ragged. Her heart thudded out tired beats.

He released her, and she fell back hard to the rocky floor. Every bone in her body screamed out in pain.

He loomed above her, seeming taller than he had been, taller but younger somehow. His skin *shone*. His eyes glittered bright as gimlets in the darkness.

"Your wish is granted," he whispered to her, and his voice hurt her ears.

She wanted to rise, wanted to shout at this man who suddenly seemed less than a man, somehow...or something more.

She wanted to help her sister.

But she could not move; she was too weak. The White Monk smiled at her, smiled at her and turned away.

Catherine watched helpless as he advanced on Jayne. He towered over her. She scowled up at him.

"And now for the real delicacy," he whispered.

"What have you done to Catherine?" Jayne demanded.

"Only what she asked for, my sweet one," the White Monk purred, "No more nor less. And now...why don't you give your brave little friend a kiss? He likes you, you know!"

Even in the gloom of the cave, Catherine could see that the meaning of the White Monk's words were not lost on George: the boy was blushing, bright as blood.

"Oh, don't be so coy, boy!" the White Monk sounded almost friendly, but his eyes flashed, green and cold, "You want to kiss her, don't you? Answer me."

George swallowed, then, "Yes," he stammered, "Yes, she's beautiful."

"Of course she is!" exclaimed the White Monk, sounding delighted, "And she'll be more beautiful too – we'll see, you can be sure of it! That is the gift, the great gift that has been given to all the children of men: before the withering and the dust comes the flowering, for ever and ever and ever. Such beauty! Such *life*! All the stars that ever were could never burn so brightly."

Catherine swallowed, tried to speak.

"No," she croaked, but her voice was horse and her words were lost before they were spoken.

"Now," said the White Monk, and his voice and his face and his whole body was cold and terrible, "Now: kiss!"

George hesitated, took a step towards Jayne, stopped. Jayne did not move.

"Now!" the White Monk cried again; and faster than Catherine could follow, his arms shot out. One hand grabbed George behind the neck, the other found Jayne.

With easy strength he forced the children together.

"Kiss."

Jayne hesitated, and gave George a peck on the cheek.

The White Man turned George's face.

They kissed.

For a moment, nothing happened.

Then it was as if a fire had sprung up inside each of them. Two beacons of light shone forth, and the luminance that shot from the children sallied out and rippled along the cold stone walls of the cave, flickering and burning and writhing in the shadows.

Then the quality of the light changed: from yellow to heart-red it shone, becoming richer and darker and filled with something at once powerful and menacing and joyous. But for every ripple that reflected off the cavern walls, that ripple then turned and twisted, and fled with snake speed to the White Monk, whose hands still gripped the necks of those who kissed.

Catherine looked back to her sister, and gasped.

She looked so different she could hardly recognise her.

She had grown tall and slender, curves shimmering out of her child's body, making a woman of her. The same was happening to George: his shoulders had grown very broad, and now he was tall, so tall, as tall as the White Monk.

And then George was taller than the Monk; and Catherine realised it was not because George was growing, but rather because the Monk was shrinking. His legs were shortening, his muscular, lupine frame was turning in on itself, becoming soft and small, the body of a child.

But still the White Monk gripped Jayne's neck, gripped it tight, and forced her close to George, though from the look on her face she needed no more forcing.

Catherine gasped.

Jayne's face...what was happening to her face...?

It was melting, flesh sagging and wrinkling, hair fading from gold to gray to white as chalk.

George too: his ears and nose grew obscenely, his coal black hair flashed white and then was falling away, settling lightly on the ground then being blown away forever.

"Enough!" the White Monk's voice had changed: it was as high and shrill as befitted the child he had become. He released Jayne and George, and a dry gasp escaped their lips.

The once-were-children fell to their knees.

Catherine reached out for her sister. Jayne sought her with clouded eyes. Their gazes locked, and Catherine stumbled forward.

She grasped her sister's withered hand; and it was only then that she realised her own hand looked the same: dry and crumpled and broken and *old*.

Jayne blinked at her.

Jamie Brindle

"I'm sorry," Catherine groaned. She wanted to shout it, to roar it out, but all that came was a moan, a sad old moan.

Jayne shook her head.

"Red," she muttered, "The Red Man. He could help..."

"NO!" shouted the White Monk, "You are mine, not his, MINE! And I...will have...the last...of YOU!"

And with that he seized Jayne again in one hand, and George in the other and...

                    ...*squeezed*...

...and suddenly Catherine was screaming as she saw the withered scraps of flesh on her sister curl in to themselves and fall to dust on the cavern floor.

All that was left were the bones.

The White Monk shoved and the skeletons flew backwards into the stone wall, where they lodged and froze and looked for all the world as if they had been there since the world began.

He turned to Catherine and fixed his icy child's smile on her.

"Pretty flowers," he whispered, "Pretty flowers but Oh! So briefly do they bloom..."

He reached for her.

But Catherine suddenly found she had some reserve, some desperate energy she had no knowledge of until she had this last need of it. She

176

stumbled to her feet, ducked out of the way of his lashing hand, and found herself abruptly in the open air.

How long she had been in the cave she could not guess; but night had come, and in the sky the pale moon and stars shone bright over the eternal rocks and trees that swayed forever in the wind.

He was behind her.

He reached for her.

Down the cairn she tumbled, throwing herself over and tumbling, heedless of old bones and bruises that she could no longer heal.

She reached the bottom, panting and in pain. She looked up. He was above her, his white cassock shimmering beautiful in the moonlight, silver and magic and deathly.

She staggered to her feet.

Onwards, away.

Onwards, away.

Her mind was not working as it should, she could tell. Nothing in her old body worked as it should.

She reached the tarn. He was following, languidly, taking his time.

He laughed, and his laughter was silver, too, and cold, and mixed with the moonlight and the freezing water and the song of the wind in the trees.

Onwards, away.

Onwards, away.

She reached the narrowing of the path, felt the brambles tearing at her skin again as she brushed past them.

He drifted after her, smoke and silver.

Onwards, away.

She reached the second clearing, with it's striated veins of jutting stones.

His child's breath was on her neck, his white cassock was catching under her feet.

Onwards, away.

She reached the rough wall of the cliff, and pressed her back against it.

There was no onwards. There was no away.

"And so it comes to this, as it always does," the White Child gazed up at her with cold, inhuman eyes, "From flesh leaks the life, and the stones take the bones".

He reached for her.

Bone, she thought, and in her mind it was her sister's voice that spoke the word, *Bone and blood. White and red.*

She knew what to do.

Her hand was in her pocket.

It closed on something hard and sharp.

It was the bone she had found earlier.

She pulled it out and held it in front of her, as if to ward off the White Child.

Her hand shook feebly in the moonlight.

The boy smiled, but there was no joy in it.

"You mean to hurt *me* with *that*?" he sneered at her.

"No," she said, and stabbed her arm with the bone.

She scraped, as hard as she dared, as hard as she could, scraped and tore at the place where she had cut herself with her broken mirror, earlier that day and a million years ago.

The skin broke like paper and blood welled up. It was rich and crimson and broke the spell of moonlight, and all at once colour had returned to the world.

The White Boy froze.

"What have you DONE!" he screamed. He lunged for her...

...but another hand checked his.

"Your time is done and morning is very near,"

The Red Monk looked old, older than he had before. But there was strength in his arm.

Catherine's blood fell from her and seeped into the dust of the earth.

A bass note rumbled, so deep and awful that Catherine thought that the world itself must have broken. The ground trembled beneath her feet.

The stones shifted around her. They were shuffling themselves out of the cliff side, turning and edging and escaping and falling to the floor.

Not stone, she thought, *Bones*.

They sprawled on the ground in rough piles...twitched...spun round and formed up.

Catherine gasped. All around her, shapes were gathering from the darkness. Wolves, she recognised, many, many wolves, made of alabaster bone and bound with sinew woven up of silver moonlight mixed with a dripping, sanguine red she knew was her own. Other creatures there were too, all shapes and forms and sizes; some she knew; some were strange; some were hideous and twisted and broken.

The White Boy was backing away now. The creatures were cawing and crying and baying and shrieking for him. Skeletal bones shuffled from the rock and swooped through the leaves on wings as light as music.

The White Boy turned and fled from the terrible host.

"Come," said the Red Monk.

Catherine shook her head; it seemed she was too weary even to talk.

But he grasped her hand, and as he did so, strength seemed to flow back into her, the same strength that the White Monk had stolen.

Together, they followed the skeletal figures.

They went all in a rush and hurry, sweeping through the little path lined with brambles, and out once more into the opening by the tarn. The moon had vanished now, and the light that shimmered back from the still surface of the water was the burning oranges and purples of the coming dawn.

Still the White Boy fled, and after followed those awful creatures; until at last he stood at the bottom of the great cairn, and this he started to climb as fast as ever he could.

But the animals checked here, and stayed at the bottom of the mound. Even the skeletal birds did not try to approach the White Boy as he climbed.

Finally, he reached the top; and then he turned to face them, and triumph was on his face.

"See!" his voice sounded shrill in the emptiness, "You cannot win, you red fool! I win this time, as I always win, as I always shall win! I have proven again what I always prove: the flower is bright, but it is brief! And when it withers, all that remains is bone!"

The Red Monk looked up at the White Boy, and in the gathering light Catherine could see he was smiling.

"And yet bone remembers," he barely whispered the words, but Catherine felt sure that the White Boy heard them as clear as if they were shouted, "Bone always remembers: the brightness of the flowers and the warmth of flesh and the song of life raised in joy for the joy of life itself. Bone has returned to claim you: the bone and dust that is yours; it will always remember the blood and song which is mine."

The Red Monk gestured to the East.

"And see now: the red dawn has come!"

And at that moment the first true sunbeam of the new day broke over the mountain and roared above their heads. It struck the White Boy full on, and wreathed his white cassock in orange fire.

And behind the White Boy, it struck the mouth of the cave: the earth shook.

All turned to stillness. Catherine felt her breath catch in her throat.

With immeasurable slowness, with such awful, unbearable slowness, the mountain awoke.

The cave shuddered and heaved. Dust and rocks and shingle fell away, the cavern arched up, and behold!

The mouth of the cave was a mouth indeed, a great skeletal monstrous mouth, enormous in size and with teeth as long and sharp as swords. Huge skeletal feet thudded down, and the reptilian monster reared up and roared into the dawn, a roar of rage, of joy, of life unknown for an eternity reclaimed for one last breath.

Before the wolves came, there were others, Catherine thought, remembering, *Other creatures, large and small and fast and slow...and terrible*.

The creature heaved and writhed its gargantuan neck.

Then with a shudder it turned towards the blinking White Boy below.

Its mouth gaped wide.

It plunged downward.

Catherine had a single clear glimpse of the White Boy poised with one arm held up as if to shield his face, and then the beast was upon him, and he was gone.

Cacophony owned the world.

Dust and bones fell all around her. Catherine crouched down and tried to make herself as small as possible, sure some huge rock would hit her and kill her at any moment.

But gradually the noise subsided, and the rock never came.

She stood. The Red Monk was beside her, standing quite calmly and gazing at where the cairn and the cave and the White Boy had been. All that was there now was a cliff face, rugged and bare.

Nearby, the water of the tarn made small splashing noises as a few last pebbles rolled into the depths and disturbed the stillness.

"Is...is he dead?" she asked.

The Red Monk made a noise that was almost a chuckle.

"He always was," he answered, "He always will be. No, he is not dead – just...gone. For now."

"Oh," said Catherine.

"He has no life of his own, understand me," the Red Monk continued, "Only that which he can steal..."

And in that moment, Catherine's world fell apart: she remembered her sister.

"Jayne!" she wailed, "He took Jayne and he took George, and it was all my fault!"

She fell to the floor again, weeping.

When she next looked about, dawn had broken fully, and the Red Monk had gone.

She was thirsty from the tears, so she crawled to the side of the tarn.

She had taken four mouthfuls of the sweet, cold, fresh water before she saw her. So still she was beneath the little lapping waves of the tarn that she mistook the girl for her own reflection. But when she moved, the girl beneath the waves stayed still.

She looked so serine: not dead, just sleeping.

George was next to her. Their hands were nearly touching, shifting ever so slightly back and forth in the invisible ebb and flow of some unseen current beneath the shimmering waters.

Catherine leaned in closer, hardly daring to breath.

Then she realised there was someone standing over her. She could see him reflected in the water. His red cassock shifted in the wind. She met his eyes, and for a moment it almost seemed he was smiling at her.

She kneeled down, and felt something sharp press into her knee. Her arm stung suddenly where she had cut it yesterday.

Yes, the Red Monk seemed to whisper.

"Catherine!"

The shout echoed across the clearing. It was her mother.

"Catherine! Where have you *been*! We've been looking for you all night! Where are the others?" That was her father.

Catherine smiled and cut herself.

The blood burst crimson on the water.

She turned round to face her parents, bleeding and bleeding and beaming.

"Don't worry," she said, "They just fell in."

Her father caught her as she fell. She smiled.

Behind her, the water splashed, and two young children laughed for the simple joy of the living sunlight.

The End

Jamie Brindle

Handle With Care

In the beginning was the Word, and the Word was, "bugger."

In fact, if you want to be technical, the Word predated the beginning; or rather it would have done so if there had been any time to speak of prior to that point.

It's all a matter of perspective, really.

From the point of view of Bob, who was the one who had been carrying the small, pulsating sphere of crackling potential, the Word was not in the beginning, it was somewhere in the middle – the middle of his journey between where he worked and where he had been tasked to carry the strange, pulsating violet object. From his point of view, the Word was simply the word he uttered when he realised the highly unusual and – importantly – *delicate* object had slipped away form him and shattered with a disappointing little *phitzz* noise.

On the other hand, from the point of view of the small pulsating sphere of crackling potential, "bugger" was the Word which immediately predated creation.

There was an awful lot of something and an awful lot of the exact opposite, all scrunched up together very tight. This situation lasted for about as close as you can get to no time at all whilst still existing in a place where time has, for once, actually started ticking away. Then, with the abrupt springing noise of a Universe that is still getting the hang of things, the something and its exact opposite suddenly realised that they could cancel each other out, which they proceeded to do with great abandon.

All at once, there was a great deal of energy about.

After that, things were pretty much in motion.

The small amount of something that was left over (there having been slightly more of that than its exact opposite) shot out in every direction, cooling, coalescing, and generally exploring the far horizons of the expanding cosmos.

Some time after that, stars began to form.

Planets formed up out of the patchy remnants of interstellar dust, swimming into focus like cells under a microscope.

The vast majority of them were barren, lifeless things, but that still left a plethora that began knocking simple organic molecules together in interesting ways.

Things rapidly got more complicated.

Before long, little pouches of water were bumbling around, desperately trying to protect and propagate the small chains of novel organic molecules they contained, whilst simultaneously attempting to get one up on the other little bumbling pouches of water.

After that, the little pouches of water grew arms and legs and started using mobile phones, but the basic format of life had essentially been worked out.

"What do you mean, you dropped it?" demanded Quince, fixing Bob with his thousand-Watt gaze, whilst casually thrusting a Life into his latest client and betraying only the slightest hint of satisfaction as the insubstantial thing boiled away into the ether.

Bob twisted wretchedly.

"Um, well," Bob squirmed, "I didn't so much *drop* it as *not hold onto it*," he hazarded, desperately trying to avoid his employer's gaze whilst simultaneously looking him straight in the face, an endeavour which resulted only in a slow rotation.

Quince sighed. He had been having such a nice day, or he would have if such things as days existed here, in this great calm ocean of non-time within which realities nestled like coiled roses.

He had been getting on with things. Making progress.

He was always so busy, that was the problem.

There were always clients for him, *always*. He offered such a remarkable service, as he always told himself, such an important one. He really was something of a big deal.

His clients were known, in the business, as Poor Souls. As light as breath, as innocent as snow, as delicate as a daydream, these fresh-minted shades crept out of the dazzling brilliance of the Beginning and came to him, begging for his services.

And what service did he offer?

Why, what every Poor Soul needs to gain weight, of course – a life!

It was only natural that his services would be wildly popular. He was always busy.

And just when he has felt that he was starting to make real headway...

"I see," said Quince with a dangerous calmness in his voice, "And the difference between 'dropping' something and 'not holding onto it' would be what, exactly?"

"Um," tried Bob, "One of them's not my fault?"

"So where exactly did you drop it?" said Quince, peering around the disparate, loose puffs of non-space that marked the area around his realm.

Bob ducked back and forth anxiously, trying to locate the exact place where the delicate crackling sphere had fallen. There seemed to be nothing left of it at all, no shards of the pulsing shell, no lambent strands of the haunting glow from within, not even the faintest tang of ethereal potential to mark its passage.

Jamie Brindle

Then he saw it – the tiniest glimmering hint of something unworldly shimmering near the floor.

He bent to investigate it, and Quince saw where the sphere had fallen.

"Bob," said Quince, in the voice of calculated serenity which is frequently adopted by the deeply panicked, "Stay exactly where you are. Good. Now very, very slowly straighten yourself up again and back off a bit."

Bob nodded, doing as he was instructed, and Quince looked on in relief as the hugely distorted image of his underling gradually coalesced again back into its usual dimensions, shaking off the prism effect cast by the nearby remnants of the thing Bob had dropped.

Quince took a deep breath.

"Congratulations Bob," he said, "It looks like you're a God."

There is life, and there is death. What happens after death is only known by a handful of people – not counting those who have actually died, of course – and they are disinclined to discuss the matter, perhaps for contractual reasons. What happens before life, on the other hand, is known by literally everyone, or would be if they didn't have such a habit of forgetting these trivial details when confronted by the raging vibrancy of life itself.

Quince had seldom entered Life himself, however, and for this reason had a pretty solid understanding of the mechanics of before-the-cradle.

In the burning centre of this un-place, the fires of creation roared away, raw particles of consciousness spontaneously being forged from the dark essence of existence itself. These particles coalesced into Poor Souls, and went tramping their hollow footsteps across the dip and flow of empty nothing to find Quince and his never-ending stack of Lives. At this point they would leave the temporary holding-bay and flash away to whatever wonders waited beyond, gaining weight and evolving awareness with every lived experience, and edging day by day towards the mysterious farther shore.

That was where the Poor Souls originated from: the Forges of Creation. And they comprised the overwhelming majority of the entities that Quince encountered.

Occasionally, just occasionally however, something different would come his way.

They would turn up out of the blue, unexpected, luminous, pulsating things heavy with the dangerous purple crackle of unearthed potential.

A *Rich* Soul.

And the last thing Quince would do with a Rich Soul was unite it with a life.

Such acts were dangerous.

No, the correct thing to do – so Quince had learnt a *very* long time ago – was to send it back to the Beginning. Send it tumbling back into the Forges of Creation, where it would be re-forged and re-made and a thousand new Poor Souls would be re-born.

Jamie Brindle

The problem with Rich Souls was that they were so *ambitious*.

They were so full of life already, they were almost bursting at the seams.

They had to be handled with care, or who knew what might happen?

"But...but I'm not ready to be a God!" stammered Bob.

"You'd be surprised how few are, young man," said Silverlight, with a tone that seemed to imply youth was an embarrassing affliction any decent person would refrain from mentioning in polite company, except her, of course, on account of her extreme lack thereof.

Silverlight was ancient. She was older than Quince, and that was pretty hard, given that Quince was basically setting up his stall and whistling before the first Universe had a place to go Bang in.

It was Silverlight that Quince had taken Bob to see as soon as he had found out what had happened to the Rich Soul. They had found her by her endlessly burning forge, of course, with Poor Souls streaming out of the fires and away all the while.

"But I don't even know how to create eggs," Bob protested, "Quince tried to show me once – do you remember? – and that went terribly wrong! And now you're telling me I somehow managed to create a whole *Universe*!"

"Not much difference between the two, when it comes to that," mused Silverlight, "Both look very neat and smooth on the outside, but actually all

192

they are is a frightful mess waiting to get out. Also, they are both distinctly improved by toast..."

Her gaze snapped back to Bob.

"In any case," she went on, "You may not have been able to create an egg, but you were at least instrumental in creating a Universe. And since you were the last being to touch it before it burst, that makes you its de facto God."

"But...but, I don't know the first thing about being a God!"

"Oh, most of them seem to make it up as they go along," said Quince glibly, who had never got on very well with the Authorities, "I'm sure it can't be that difficult. You can fit it in around your usual duties, certainly."

"No, no, no!" scolded Silverlight, pumping her bellows for extra effect and sending a storm of raw creation spurting off into the distance, "That will *not* do! What are you suggesting, Quince? That he becomes an absentee God? Working for you most of the time and moonlighting as Lord of Creation? How typical of your generation..."

Quince, who had not previously considered himself as belonging to *any* generation, but who nevertheless had a fine ear for an insult, bristled.

"Well, then, can't he put it up for adoption?" he challenged, "There must be all sorts of little lost Gods wandering around, just wishing they had this opportunity!"

"No," said Bob, softly but with a new firmness in his voice, "I made this Universe, and I'm going to deal with it. Responsibly."

Quince looked from Bob to Silverlight, and back again.

Jamie Brindle

"Fine!" he blustered at last, "If that's the way you feel, then I should probably be going! Seeing as how busy I'm going to be *without an assistant*!"

He turned and stalked away.

"And don't come crying to me when your Universe turns round and declares it's an atheist!" he shouted back at them.

"Don't mind him," said Silverlight gently, "He's just bitter he never managed to work his way up from eggs."

Poor Souls came to Quince, as they always had; but as non-time wore on, he found he was struggling to keep up. He had always been busy, but now things were getting ridiculous.

"One life, please," a client would breath, and as he was busy rummaging beneath his desk for the first Life to come to hand, Quince would find himself hemmed in by three more Souls that had crept up on him unawares.

"What happens in this one?"

"Do I get to do great things?"

"How long do I live for?"

The questions poured over him, ceaseless and searching; and while previously he had felt invulnerable, on the top of his game, always ready to

194

answer these questions with a flash of charm and an unerring salesmanship, now he felt the quality of his work was beginning to slide.

"Er, this life?" he hazarded, trying to buy time, "Um, very special life, this one. You, um, raise the standards."

"I see. And which standards would those be?" the Poor Soul would parry, polite but obviously not convinced.

"Oh, you know, just general standards," Quince would flap, already thinking of the next client, and the next, and the one after that, "They were rather low before you come along. Then they, um, get higher..."

And he would spin the Life towards the sceptical Soul with a desperate little flick, and both would vanish off into existence in a puff of vague dissatisfaction.

Eventually, Quince felt that things had gone too far.

This would simply not do!

After all, he was a craftsman, an expert, an artiste!

He would not allow the quality of his work to suffer, simply because his assistant suddenly felt he had better things to do, such as playing nursemaid to a fledgling Universe that was probably perfectly capable of looking after itself...

Ignoring the jostling mass of Poor Souls – there seemed to be more of them then ever – he hung a little sign in the blank nothing above his desk.

The sign read:

Jamie Brindle

GONE TO TALK WITH GOD

ON URGENT BUSINESS

PLEASE WAIT IN THE

INFINITE SPACE PROVIDED

Shoving his way through the hollow press of Souls, Quince worked his way towards where he knew Bob's little Universe had sprung up.

But it was only when he realised that the line of Poor Souls was coming from the very place that Quince was heading that he understood, suddenly, why he had been so busy.

The line of Poor Souls arched away from him towards a singularity of distortion, their forms hunching and fracturing kaleidoscopically the closer they got to the point from which they originated.

Bob's little Universe was being busy.

Quince growled to himself and hurried forward.

He got closer and closer to the epicentre of distortion until, with a strange *whoosh*, Quince was tugged forward...

...And felt the Universe fold around him...

...Before being deposited back in a place that was almost exactly the same, but felt *inverted*, somehow.

He shook himself, and looked around.

Now he could see that the Souls were streaming away from a small replica Beginning, brightly burning and very similar to the one which churned out the Poor Souls in his own corner of what passed, at a stretch, for reality.

He even fancied he could catch a glimpse of Silverlight working the bellows, although whether it was a separate entity that occupied this nested reality, or simply another facet of a creature that protruded into realities beyond number, he never got around to wondering, because at that moment he saw Bob.

"Tea?" offered Bob, leaning forward to indicate a little steaming pot. His golden beard shone, and on his head was a rather ostentatious silver crown.

Quince demurred, and looked around at Bob's new friends.

They looked back at him and smiled nervously.

"So, Quince," began one of them, a huge burly man with a big hammer tucked casually into his trousers, "The boss says he knows you from a some time ago, is that right?"

"Oh yes," replied Quince idly, "Bob and I go way back."

"Humph," said Bob pointedly, waggling his eyebrows.

"Oh, yes, sorry," said Quince, sounding not a bit of it, "I mean, *God* and I go way back."

Jamie Brindle

"Yes, we used to work together," Bob interjected, "Back before I decided to set out on my own."

Quince smiled blandly and made a mental note of this suggestion of equality, which he found fundamentally offensive.

"Indeed we did," he said, and looked around the assembled minor deities, before fixing his gaze on the creature that had addressed him, "And what do you do, my good being?" he asked.

"He's in charge of thunder!" explained Bob proudly.

"Are you now?" grinned Quince, "How splendid! And do you specialise in making bodies of air rush together in particular, or do you branch out into, oh you know, conducting electricity to the ground, precipitation of rainwater, that sort of thing?"

The poor deity looked into Quince's smile and was very aware that it was composed mainly of teeth.

"Oh, he does all sorts!" Bob cut in, "We all do! That's the beauty of the system! That's why I created all of them! It really gives the people something to, you know, something to believe in!"

Quince nodded.

"I see, I see," he said, "Well, you do seem to be getting on rather well here. Anyway, as nice as it is to have a little, ah, chit chat, I have in fact come here on business."

"Really?" said Bob, adopting a guarded air, "And what business is that?"

198

"Why, *our* business, of course!" exclaimed Quince, "The truth is, things are getting rather busy, what with all these new lives of yours. Now, I'm sure you've had fun getting things going here, but now that the system's up and running, as it were, isn't it time you came back to your real job?"

Bob's expression darkened.

"Oh, no, no!" he said, "Not a chance! I'm sorry, but I couldn't possibly. I'm so frightfully busy, you see," he leaned in, "Between you and me, the Universe is still a bit of a handful."

"What do you mean?" said Quince, "It's a *Universe*! It's *meant* to be a handful!"

"Yes, yes I know," replied Bob, "But, well, first of all, there's the sheer *size* of the place. I keep finding bits I hadn't noticed before. And that doesn't look good if you're meant to be omniscient."

"Well, all the more reason to pack it in and downsize to something more manageable," tried Quince.

"No, no, I *can* manage it!" snapped Bob, "Anyway," he went on more calmly, "That's not the worst of it. The worst is the *people*. I turn my back for one moment and you can be sure they're getting up to something."

"Like what?" asked Quince, genuinely interested despite himself.

"Well, for instance, the other day I decided to have a little get together. Nothing fancy, you know, bit of music, bit of dancing, roast some marshmallows on the fire, that sort of thing."

Quince nodded.

"Only thing is, some cheeky bugger gets wind of it, decides to sneak up here and nick the fire!" said Bob, unable to keep the hurt out of his voice.

"Some people," muttered Quince.

"I know!" agreed Bob, "Now they've got fire years, *millennia* before they were meant to! Nothing good will come of it, mark my words. And I had to punish the thief of course, poor sod."

"Really? How did you do that?"

"Oh, I created a special Vengeful God," Bob beamed, clearly pleased with himself.

A vast, ugly creature away to one side waved at Quince.

"It does sound very stressful," Quince nodded, an idea suddenly forming, "Well, I imagine your time is very precious, and I've taken up enough of it."

"Are you going?" said Bob reluctantly, "But you could at least stay and have a bit of a look around. There are some wonderful views. There's a particularly stunning galaxy being formed in this nice, quiet little corner of creation, if you fancy? Or you could see some of my crew at work if you want?"

Quince smiled. That had been exactly what he had been hoping for.

"Well, I suppose I *am* quite intrigued to see what a Vengeful God gets up to," purred Quince, "Perhaps you could introduce us?"

"Certainly!" beamed Bob, and led Quince over to where the vast ugly creature was lurking.

"Now I really must dash," said Bob, "But it was lovely to see you! Please see yourself out when you've finished talking. And do pop in again!"

And with that, Bob was gone.

"So," said Quince, turning to the ghastly apparition before him, "I suppose you find your work satisfying?"

"Well, you could say that," said the creature, gristly sheets of chitin sliding over tightly bunched muscles, "To be honest with you, there are times it gets rather samey."

"Oh dear," said Quince, putting an arm round the vast creature, as far as it would stretch, at least, "You must remember, there's always room at the top for a talented young God with bold ideas..."

It didn't take long for Quince to say all he felt he needed to say. Then he shook the creature by one huge bloody hand, nodded to the rest of the assembled deities, and concentrated hard.

He felt the Universe bunch around him...

...There was a tickling sensation...

...And with a feeling that the Universe had sneezed around him, Quince was expectorated back into his own reality.

He sauntered jauntily back towards his desk. He felt sure that things were in motion. All he had to do was wait.

But the Poor Souls kept on coming. Despite an initial calming in their numbers, they soon picked up again, and Quince eventually had to face the fact that his plan, as promising as it had seemed, had failed.

Lives kept bubbling up from under his desk quicker than ever before, and it was all he could do to lob them as fast they could surface into the Souls that crowded round him, tighter and tighter and tighter still.

At length, he decided there was nothing for it but to visit Bob again.

The Poor Soul floated through the void and up to Quince.

"Hello," it said gently, "I would like one life, please."

"Hello," said Quince.

There was a pause.

"Yes, hello," repeated the Soul, who was almost completely incapable of impatience or irritation, "I have come here in search of a life. Perhaps you could help me?"

"Hello," said Quince, flickering slightly, "We apologise, but our service is very busy at the moment. You are now held in a queue. We will be with you as soon as possible."

"Oh, I see," mumbled the Poor Soul, as the flickering simulacrum of Quince began to hum annoyingly.

Non-time passed.

"I'm sorry," repeated Quince, apropos of nothing, "You are held in a queue. For your information, this conversation is being recorded for quality and training and intimidation purposes. Please feel free to hum along while you wait."

The humming persisted.

"I'm sorry," said Quince again, "You are held in a queue. Your business is nominally important to us. So we can direct you to the most appropriate service, please tell us now what service you require."

"Life," said the Soul, the faintest tinge of exasperation creeping into its voice.

"I'm sorry," said the Quince-thing with crushing banality, "We didn't quite catch that. Did you say, 'chips'?"

"No, not 'chips', 'life'!" shouted the Soul.

"You have selected 'Chips'," intoned Quince, beaming, "We hope you enjoy your choice, and look forward to your business in the eternity to follow."

There was a tingling sensation, an ominous gurgling noise, and a small puff of vapour.

A slightly grubby-looking egg hung benignly in the ether.

"Sod this," mumbled the Poor Soul, before spontaneously dissolving into its component elements with a terminal little *phth* sound.

The demonically smiling Quince-thing hummed away to itself in a void that was rapidly becoming rather less voidy and distinctly more eggish.

Meanwhile, the real Quince made his way back to Bob's little Universe. Once again he found the source of distortion; once again he pushed into it...

...and popped out into the little nested cosmos...

...only to find Bob's domain had changed somewhat since his last visit.

The most striking thing was the emptiness. A few wisps of cloud skittered through the grand, hollow hall; and in the middle of the hall, all alone and without any other gods to attend him, stood Bob.

He looked a little older, a little thicker around the waist, and his previously yellow beard was now bushier and stark white. But it was Bob.

Quince sauntered over to him.

"Hello, Bob," he said, "Thought I'd pop back and see how the God business is going?"

"What?" said Bob, looking momentarily irked, before his eyes swam up and took Quince in, "Oh, Quince!" he exclaimed, "You took me by surprise there!"

Bob grasped Quince's hand in a distracted fashion, gave him a perfunctory smile, and went back to the business of staring rather hard at nothing in particular.

Silence stretched out between them.

"Um, yes," said Quince at length, somewhat off-balance, "Well, I just happened to be passing, as it were, and I thought I might drop in, you know, for old time's sake..."

"I see, I see," muttered Bob, not looking at him. A few beads of sweat formed on his brow and ran down his cheek, "The thing is Quince, I am most dreadfully busy..."

"Really?" said Quince, "Busy doing, um, what, exactly?"

"Oh, you know," said Bob vaguely, "Watching. Judging. Smiting the unbelievers. The usual Godly racket. Ah, got one!"

A brief smile flashed across his face.

"Worshiping a graven image, eh?" He muttered darkly, almost to himself, "These poor schmucks never learn, you know..."

Quince shifted slightly.

"Worshiping a what?" he asked.

"Oh, you know," Bob flapped a hand, "Worshiping a carving. Rather than, ahem, yours truly."

"Not fond of graven images, then?" asked Quince.

"Oh, no!" exclaimed Bob, shaking his head vigorously, "Can't stand graven images, me. If there's one thing I hate, it's gravening!"

"I see..." said Quince gently, whilst wondering in a general way about how good extended periods of time in a position of absolute authority were for the maintenance of sanity, "Well, you do seem to be rather busy...what happened to all your, er, hired help?"

Bob darted Quince a sharp look.

"Couldn't trust them," He said at length, "Sneaky little buggers, each and every one of 'em."

Quince nodded in a non-committal way.

"Actually," went on Bob, blinking a few times and wondering idly whether it was about time for a burnt offering or two, "It wasn't long after you last popped in. They began to get ideas above their station. Wanted a bigger piece of the pie, as it were. Couldn't be doing with that. So they had to go."

"They had to go?" repeated Quince.

"Oh yes, they had to go," went on Bob, while making a little pass with his hand and absent-mindedly creating a moderate-sized plague of lotuses, "It was nice as an experiment, you know, polytheism. But it's really not the future."

"Is it not?" commented Quince gloomily, who had taken rather a shine to the special Vengeful God, and had nurtured fond hopes that it might even have been able to overthrow Bob and thus get him his assistant back, "What is the future, then?"

"Oh, *mono*theism, no doubt about it!" exclaimed Bob, enthusiasm bubbling in his voice, "It's a lot of work, but I'm quite sure it'll pay dividends! All you have to do is, see, you pick a group of people and manifest yourself in front of them, as, oh I don't know, a glowing tiger, or a...a huge, monstrous man, or a...a burning bush or something!"

"A burning bush?" asked Quince sceptically.

"Oh, you'd be surprised what works, believe me!" affirmed Bob, "Anyway, you manifest yourself, and say something along the lines of, 'Oi, you buggers, stop what you're doing and listen to me! I'm the boss round here, the one and only *true* boss, and you lot are the chosen people. So you better do what I say...'"

"...Like, for example, no gravening..." cut in Quince.

"...Yes, absolutely, no bloody gravening," went on Bob, "And whilst you're at it, Johnny Foreigner over in the next valley has some rather strange ideas about not eating grapes on a Thursday or chopping the end of their winkles off or whatever, and you better sort that nonsense out pronto like, or else!'"

"I see," nodded Quince, "And they listen to you, do they?"

"Well, by and large, yes!" went on Bob, "But listen, this is the clever bit: what you do next is, you go and see Johnny Foreigner over in the next valley, and this time you manifest yourself as, oh, say an eight-armed purple monkey or something, and say, 'Right now listen here, I'm the boss, and what I says goes, right, and you are the chosen people, and I want you to refrain from eating grapes on a Thursday and chop the end of your winkles off, got me?'"

"But why would you do that?" asked Quince, "That's just going to make all these different people want to kill each other!"

"Exactly!" beamed Bob happily, "That's the whole point, don't you see? Nothing makes for tighter unity than a good, effective enemy figure! Pumps up the selection pressure, too, gets an arms race going. You'd be amazed how quickly things have been progressing since I switched

Jamie Brindle

theological models. They've been inventing all sorts of clever things since you were last here!"

"Like what?" asked Quince suspiciously.

"Oh, you know, lots of things," said Bob vaguely, "Spears, bows, catapults. Vices, racks, hot irons. *Lots* of different kinds of swords! The list goes on..."

"Yes, and it seems to consist mainly of sharp, unpleasant things," said Quince, with narrowed eyes.

Bob shifted slightly.

"And what, pray, do you mean by that?" said Bob coldly.

Quince, who had never thought of Bob as the kind of person who could use the word, 'pray' in a sentence, suddenly found himself wondering how much his assistant had changed.

"Well, it seems like a pretty low way for a god to behave, that's all," muttered Quince, "Next you'll be telling me you've promised them an afterlife or something!"

Bob managed to hide the brief embarrassed look after only a moment, but it was enough.

"Oh, Bob, you haven't!" exclaimed Quince, "That only ends up confusing the poor buggers when they find out what Level Two is *actually* about..."

"Shut up!" shouted Bob, advancing on Quince and raising an arm threateningly, "This is *my* Universe, and I'll run it how *I* see fit!"

"Now, wait a minute Bob, just stay calm..." protested Quince as he was backed towards a desk in one corner of the grand hall.

"Calm!" shouted Bob, "I'll give you calm! You never showed me the respect I deserved! *Never*! Maybe it's time I gave *you* a little smiting..."

Bob reached into one voluminous sleeve and pulled out a wickedly glittering bolt of lightning. He pulled his arm back over his shoulder, readying the furiously spitting spear of light...

Quince reached desperately under the desk. It was a nice desk. It was, in fact, rather similar to the desk he had in his own realm. He hoped fervently that he could still perform the function here that he had performed elsewhere across the whole of eternity.

His fingers grasped a familiar object. He had the briefest sense of the vagaries and triumphs contained within.

Quince thrust the object out so that it connected with Bob.

There was a sudden, blinding flash of light.

Bob and the life Quince had grasped both boiled away in a puff of raw creation.

There was warmth here and comfort, and Bob had the vague feeling that he was forgetting something important, something that he had been about to do, until the vivid strangeness of this new world overcame him, forcing memory and identity and everything but *now* from his mind, and emptying him out suddenly into the cold terrifying realms beyond, where harshness quickly became commonplace, a part of the known order of things, and it was only in quiet moments or queer moments when a strange feeling of *knowing* would overtake him, a peace and a certainty that this world was not the only world, that this life was but a shadow life, and all suffering shadow-suffering, unnecessary and meaningless, but for many years he did not share these thoughts, barely acknowledged them even to himself as he grew older and saw more clearly and wondered at the shocking brutality of the world, until there came a time when it was as if all the orbits of his being had swung suddenly into alignment and he knew that there was a God and that he was God and was within God and God was all and he laughed and laughed until the tears came, and then the followers came, and then at last the grim people came, and they did not like his words (though he realised, of course, that this did not matter) nor his looks and especially did not like his ideas, but what they *did* like were nails and wire and wood, cutting and binding and blood-letting and blood, and so it was that the sun set on his rude life one last time, and when he died he wore a smile with his tears.

Bob tumbled out of the other end of the life, and rolled to a stop at Quince's feet.

"Oh dear," he said, shaking himself, "I feel rather strange..."

He pulled himself to his feet and staggered over to lean against the desk nearby.

Quince was brushing his hands against one another with an overwhelming air of self-satisfaction.

"Really?" he inquired innocently, "I wonder why that is?"

"I had the strangest..." Bob began, stopped, then went on, "No, it wasn't a dream..."

The colour drained from his face.

"All I asked them to do was *love* each other, for, um, well for My sakes!" his voice creaked with disbelief, "And they bloody *killed* me!"

"Just following orders, I'm sure," said Quince sweetly, "I mean, you didn't do anything *sinful* did you? Like eat grapes on a Thursday, or cut, well, cut anything off?"

"But...but it was so *obvious*," murmured Bob, "All this fighting and killing and whatnot...it's all so *pointless*..."

"How about the gravening?" asked Quince with narrowed eyes.

"Well, now that you come to mention it, even that whole business seemed a bit, sort of, petty..."

That was enough. Quince was convinced.

"I've been a bit of a monster, haven't I?" said Bob softly.

"There, there don't be harsh on yourself," said Quince, putting an arm around Bob, and starting to lead him gently away, "I'm sure most Gods go through the smiting-and-plague phase. The terrible two thousands. Anyway, now that you've had your fill of playing at being God, why don't you just come back with me, to your nice old *comfortable* job..."

"No," said Bob.

Quince stopped.

"What?" he asked, unbelieving "You mean after all this, you're still not ready to come back to work with me?"

Bob shook his head.

"I can't," he said, "Not after what I've done to them. I have to make it up. Make it better. Wait a moment..."

He took on a glazed look as he gazed into his domain.

"I don't believe it!" Bob exclaimed, eyes swimming back into focus, "They've only gone and founded a new bloody religion on me!"

"Oh dear," said Quince mournfully, "Not another one?"

"Yes!" shouted Bob, "And...wait a minute...yes, it's already fracturing and splitting apart! I don't *believe* these people!"

"It certainly seems they believe in you," said Quince dryly, "But at least you told them to, well, to love each other. Surely that must count for something..."

"You're right!" Bob nodded frantically, "I did...let's just check...oh, no!" His face crumpled, "Now *that's* not very loving, is it?" he moaned.

Bob slumped back down to the floor.

"What is it?" asked Quince.

Bob shook his head.

"These bloody people..." he said, "You should see the things they've been doing in my name...you know, you go the effort of undergoing a messianic manifestation, tell them all exactly how it is, and you haven't been gone two millennia before it comes painfully apparent that they've completely managed to miss the whole bloody point..."

He trailed off.

Quince inspected his nails. He was pretty sure he knew where things were heading now. Perhaps there was a way out of this, after all. He would have to be quick, but he thought he could manage it.

He looked under the desk. Just as he thought, there were all the little lives, bobbing away endlessly...

He began counting.

One, two, three...

"There's only one thing for it," said Bob, surging up with a sudden resolve.

"Oh yes?" asked Quince innocently, "What's that?"

"A Second Coming!" pronounced Bob grandly.

"Really?" clucked Quince, "What does one of them involve?"

"Oh, it's simple!" said Bob enthusiastically, "You're just going to have to send me down there again, put me inside another human life, just like you did before!"

"How interesting!" purred Quince, "I completely hadn't considered that! But now that you mention it, it *does* sound like a good idea, doesn't it?"

Bob nodded furiously.

"Well, then, lets see what we've got here..." said Quince, and pulled out one of the lives from under the desk. He held himself ready. The timing would have to be exact...

"Yes, yes, that's the ticker!" said Bob, "Just pass that this way, will you?"

"Certainly, my good God," said Quince, smiling like a shark.

He thrust the life into Bob's waiting hands...

...And at exactly the same moment, he *tickled* the miniature Universe around him in exactly the right way...

There was a blinding flash of light.

The Universe sneezed.

Quince stood alone in the empty void of what he thought of, for simplicities sake, as the *real* empty void.

Something small and heavy rested in his hand.

It was spherical and dangerous and pulsated with a purplish sheen of crackling potential.

It also smelt distinctly of Bob.

Quince hummed happily to himself as he carried – with great care – the pulsating Rich Soul towards the place where it should have been taken to begin with.

He found Silverlight pumping the bellows, as she always was.

"Hello, sis'," he said, flashing her a smile.

"Hello, Quince," Silverlight answered, "So you worked out how to put the egg back in the shell, eh?"

Quince nodded.

"And now you want me to recycle it, just like the others?"

"Well," said Quince, "If you could recycle *most* of it, that would be perfect. I'm very busy, as you know."

Silverlight nodded.

"Aren't we all, my dear?" she muttered.

Silverlight reached out and grasped the Rich Soul. She pulled it close and, for a moment, gave it her full attention.

"This *was* an interesting one," she muttered, "The Poor Soul that grew into this one must really have had some strange experiences..."

The Rich Soul sparkled, and deep in its glittering depths the eternal echoes of countless reciprocal Lives and Universes shimmered out at them.

Then she shifted her weight and slid the sphere against the endless shower of sparks that leapt from her burning forge.

She pumped the bellows.

The Rich Soul shimmered and cracked.

Jamie Brindle

A wind whistled out, pushed against Quince, whispered to him of dreams and hopes and deaths and loves; a thousand incandescent images burnt through him, ghost-echoes of the consciousnesses being remade.

There was a vast cracking sound.

The Rich Soul fractured; in its place, an endless empty abundance of Poor Souls (or perhaps they were Souls that were only *very nearly* Poor) sprang away into the distance, and joined a line heading away from the bright forges and into lands that Quince new well.

One other thing remained, dazed in a heap on the ground.

"Hello Bob," said Silverlight, reaching down and pulling him upright.

Bob wavered slightly.

"Um," he said, "Hello."

"Excellent, young man!" exclaimed Silverlight, "Under the circumstances, I would count that as a sterling attempt at communication!"

"Where am I?" he inquired at length.

"You know," said Silverlight philosophically, "It's quite possible to drive oneself barmy with such questions. My advice is to be content with, 'here', and not to worry about it too much."

"Come on Bob," said Quince, waving goodbye to Silverlight and guiding his assistant away from the Forges of Creation, "I have a feeling that we're going be rather busy..."

Epilogue

"Hello," said Bob, "You look very familiar."

"Hello," said the Quince-thing, "I am sorry, we are very busy at the moment…"

Quince picked up an egg and threw it at the simulacrum.

There was an unhappy buzzing noise.

"*Splutter cough* you have selected, 'chips'," creaked the dying Quince-thing, "Thank you for *Malfunction! Malfunction!* doing business with us, and we look forward to your custom in subsequent realities…"

The next egg split the Quince-thing clean in half.

The End

Jamie Brindle

Afterword

When I read a book of short stories, I love it when the author says a few words about each story, maybe about where that story came from, or what it meant to them. What I don't like, however, is when the explanation comes at the beginning of the book; I'd much rather read it at the end, after I've read the stories and am familiar with them.

So I think I'm going to use this afterword to indulge in a little bout of naval-gazing, and if you think it arrogant of me, then I can only apologize and suggest you put the book down, these last few pages unread.

The Big Deal started with the title, bizarrely enough. I got to thinking about what the biggest deal ever could possibly be, and the story flowed from that: the deal a soul might make with a salesman when he arranges a ride on a life. I didn't understand the story fully until I had completed quite a lot of it, just wrote it one paragraph at a time, by touch, until I suddenly realised what had to happen, and how Quince would get there. If I ever get worried about death, the thought of Quince or a large, benign-looking being waiting for me at Level Two is rather comforting.

I was listening to the songs of an old, good friend of mine (his alias is kingbee, not the band, but the artist, and I'm sure you can find his music online), and the title of one of his songs, **Skeleton Jack**, sounded rather wonderful to me; I thought it deserved a story. The song is about a junkie, but the character in this story is something else. I wanted to write something with the feel of a folk tale, that read as if someone was talking to you, speaking the words aloud. I don't know how much I succeed in that, but it was lots of fun to write.

Organic Produce came about because I was in a bad mood and wanted to write something brooding and unpleasant. I didn't know, when I started it, whether it would be a supernatural story or not; reading it again now, I'm still not entirely sure. This story is notable for me in that it is the only time (so far) that I have completely forgotten where (and more disturbingly, *when*) I was while writing. I was so engrossed in it, when I heard a faint noise from outside (I usually write with earplugs in) for several seconds I could not remember if I was in Warwick or Sussex or Bedfordshire, if it was 2010 or 1998. That sounds dramatic, but I swear it's true. The feeling passed, and thankfully, so did the story; I am happy with it, but it is a bit nasty.

I Want To Believe is another story that is linked to a close friend. The real Matt (rarely Matthew) was (is?) a bit of an expert UFOlogist, and I felt he deserved a story, too. It's all rather daft, but I loved writing the aliens – it became a challenge to fit as many appendages in as I could; and I am very fond of Moses, too. Incidentally, Mathew's nemesis, Philip Frogmore, is based on another close friend – he stars in his own story, and hopefully, one day that one might be published, too.

My brother Dan did sociology at A-level, and brought me back stories of a strange way of classifying body types into three groups, but **The Mesomorph** was the one that stuck. I thought it sounded like a breed of troll, or something that was once human that was now something else.

Jamie Brindle

I couldn't leave Quince alone. I wanted to go back to him, to see what he was up to, I was sure he had more tricks to tell. I wrote the first three paragraphs of **The Other Option**, and then promptly ran out steam, and abandoned the idea as a bad one. A year later, someone sent me an email asking to translate The Big Deal into Turkish, and it reminded me of the unfinished sequel, only this time, I realised, I suddenly knew what would happen. It's funny how your brain chips away at things in the background; you don't even know it's doing anything, then suddenly it taps you on the shoulder and hands you a nearly-finished sculpture, winks, and buggers off to get some sleep. I was doing a lot of revision for medical school exams at the time, and I think the idea of being able to rest in complete nothingness – as offered by Soul Dog – was a seductive one, even if Quince disagreed. I wanted to give Quince a foil, too, which was where Bob came in. I love Bob. He's so innocent, he almost makes up for Quince being such a sly toerag.

Echoes is the more straight-laced story I mentioned in the introduction, and I hope I haven't bored you with it too much. It's essentially true, in the sense that some of the details are muddled or mixed up in time or place – even some of the larger ones – but the essence of the story feels true to me. I was interested in the way traits and experiences and ways of behaving and roles and thoughts and, well, everything seem to echo down the generations, coming up again and again; and about the roles we make for ourselves, and the roles in which we cast one another, and the ways in which a family relates to itself.

I used to work on a stroke ward, and the issue of **Advance Directives** used to come up again and again. I got to wondering about what the ultimate form of advance directive might be in some far-flung future (or maybe not so far flung...things are progressing quickly). In a sense, this story follows on from Echoes, as well, in that it is the story of a family trying to come to terms with a death, albeit an impending one.

His Hungry Little Children was another nasty little story that came out of being in a bad mood. This one was more fun to write, though not as interesting. I don't know if the father of the little creatures is an alien or a monster or some strange breed of bipedal insect, but I think I'm more worried now than I used to be, when a blister comes up on my body. The only other thing to mention is the food. Harry's ransacking of his fridge and cupboards, scoffing down flour and salad cream and eggs, this is plucked straight from a game we used to play as children, "The Gross Food Eating Game", where contestants had to progress through a series of zones, taking it in turns to eat raw, disgusting foods, and trying not to vomit. So maybe, then, the hungry little children were us.

I had a story published in an anthology called Dark Distortions, and the editor kindly asked for a "creepy monk story" that could be included in the follow up anthology the next year. **Red In Tooth And Claw** is a phrase I find very evocative and powerful; and I found it (though not for the first time) in In Memorium, a poem with which I fell in love some years ago and memorized large chunks of, and with which I still annoy my friends by reciting to this day. Anyway, it wasn't that line, but rather another couple of stanzas that sparked on this story. When my brother and I were little, our father used to tell us stories that he would make up out of thin air. Most of them I've forgotten, but one included the ghosts of dinosaurs coming out of the hills at dusk, and haunting children who went walking at

Jamie Brindle

twilight. That one has never left me, and those ghosts found a home here, saving Catherine from the White Monk and from her own mistakes. The unfortunate epilogue is that *Dark Distortions* sadly never ran to a second anthology. But I was glad for the prompting to write this story, wherever it makes its home in the end.

I didn't start off trying to write about him this time, but Quince came back again. I had an idea for a story in which a whole Universe could be held in a soul; and that when that soul was cracked open, all the Universe would spill out, so one would have to **Handle With Care**. But when I began to wonder about who would be carrying the soul when it was dropped, I realised suddenly that it was Bob, and I'd say this story belongs just as much to Bob as it does to Quince. I had a lot of fun tracing a quick evolution from polytheism to monotheism and then blowing it all up with an inverted sneeze of the Universe. I'm sure Quince and Bob will be back at some point; I just like them too much not to wonder what they might be up to.

Once again, thank you for reading these stories.

If you feel like you liked them enough to want to know when the next collection is available, please drop me a line at the website - http://thefreebook.moonfruit.com/ - and I'll add your name to the mailing list.

Until next time...

Printed in Great Britain
by Amazon.co.uk, Ltd.,
Marston Gate.